KAIJUNAUT

DOUG GOODMAN

SEVERED PRESS
HOBART TASMANIA

KAIJUNAUT

Copyright © 2017 Doug Goodman
Copyright © 2017 by Severed Press

WWW.SEVEREDPRESS.COM

ISBN: 978-1-925597-53-0

"Why does Rice play Texas?"

-John F. Kennedy

For my Dad, who would trade stories with me on the long trips between Lubbock and Austin and Tulsa. Thanks for helping me grow not just as a person, but as a storyteller.

CHAPTER ONE: CRASHING INTO THE COSMOS

1

"This is totally ridiculous. I'm gonna die."

Cole followed his wife, Emily, and C.C. into the DSMU dock. He hoped he wouldn't die. He didn't want to die. He had so much to live for: a beautiful and highly intelligent wife, his family, his xenolinguistic studies, and a vintage collection of Edgar Rice Burroughs books. Maybe it wasn't a life for everyone, but it was one he enjoyed, and he didn't like the idea of how dying would negatively impact his ability to enjoy that life.

The rest of the crew, Mathieu and Anna, were already in the dock and suited up in their Advanced eXploration Environmental Survival (AXES) suits. The closed-in room was full of large, floor-to-ceiling, white-and-black domed structures set into concave platforms. Cole thought they looked like giant dinosaur eggs set into satellite dishes.

The airlock shut and sealed behind them. From this point forward, there was only one way out of this room: exploding out of the spacecraft.

Cole took a deep breath. He pulled on his AXES suit. The AXES suits were full-body suits with protective padding for the joints. They also came with a full-filtration helmet and a small distiller tank. Each suit was highlighted in bright blue markings.

Emily said, "Take it easy, baby. This will be just like the simulators."

"I failed the simulators."

"How do you fail the simulator?" C.C. asked. "Isn't it autonomous? You press a button and then you sit back."

Anna said, "Cole pressed the wrong button and ejected himself from the EDLS before we left the ship."

"Oh, that's right…"

"Ignore them," Emily said. "You'll be fine."

"Right. Except for the part where I'm about to be jettisoned out of a ship that is itself orbiting an alien planet at about, what—six and a half kilometers per second? That's three hundred ninety kilometers per minute, which is roughly twenty three thousand kilometers an hour."

"Twenty three thousand forty, to be exact," Mathieu added.

"Twenty three thousand four hundred," Emily corrected.

"You and numbers," Cole said to Emily.

"You and letters."

Emily continued. "Taking into account the DSMU's burn rate, that means in the low gravity of the planet, the thrust-to-weight ratio is roughly 500:1. It is the safest landing possible. See, if you have a problem, you do the math, and the math will solve it."

"Erratic winds, alien planet with an unstable atmosphere. My words trump your math."

"I thought you were looking forward to this, hey" Mathieu said. "'Exploration is the destiny of mankind,' you said."

"I am. I'm just not looking forward to being dropped into an alien planet's upper atmosphere." He rubbed his stomach.

"Did you take the antacid?" Emily asked.

Cole nodded. "But I'm not sure it was enough."

"You're cute when you're nervous. Do you need help into the EDLS?"

He shook his head. Emily kissed him tenderly. For a brief moment, he held her lips to his, like he could hold her safe and close to him. Like he could hold their lives together.

She pushed away and crossed the room to her Entry, Descent, and Landing Shell (EDLS), where she pulled herself into the polished metal structure. Like butterflies reverse-engineering themselves into their cocoons, the astronauts pulled themselves into the domed EDL structures.

"This way to the EDLS, sir," JEVS said to Cole. JEVS, which was short for "JPL EVA System," was the robot custodian of the Anchor while the astronauts were away.

"Thank you, JEVS."

Cole had a little more trouble than his compatriots with climbing backwards into the EDLS. Granted, he hadn't had half their training.

"Here we sit like birds in the wilderness," C.C. sang. "Birds in the wilderness, birds in the wilderness! Here we sit like birds in the wilderness, waiting on Cole Thomas Musgrove."

While the others chuckled, JEVS buckled Cole into his seat in the DSMU. Cole shot back, "I'm late cause I got to kiss the commander. She's a damn good kisser, by the way."

"Stop it," Emily said.

Cole said, "I want that on the record before we plummet into history, or to death. My wife's a damn good kisser and I would follow her to the ends of the galaxy if she asked."

"Got it," C.C. said while the rest of the crew chuckled.

Emily checked the status of her equipment. The screens and joysticks were all operating normally. She stretched her arms into the DSMU's revolutionary dynamic chair. It was a multi-axis gimbal chair that allowed the user to sit in virtually any position and move freely while communicating with the DSMU.

While she completed her status checks, C.C. said, "Hey, you're not in charge yet. I'm still the commander of the Anchor."

Emily exhaled sharply. "C.C., are you going to give me any crap?" Her tone implied a cornucopia of bad things if C.C. responded incorrectly.

"Not giving you any crap, sir. Just not ready to relinquish my command, I guess." He cleared this throat and said to everyone: "Ahem. It's been three years that I've been your commander onboard the Anchor. I want you all to know that it was an honor and a pleasure serving you. Thank you for flying with Titan Space. Please place your trays in the forward upright position. Bad jokes aside, I'd like to thank Mr. Dan Deerfield, the CEO of Titan Space, as well as the board of directors, chief engineer Rick Render, and all the hard-working engineers at Titan Space and NASA who developed and tested the Anchor."

"Gracias, C.C.," Anna said.

"Yeah, thanks, man," Cole said.

"Three big cheers for C.C.," Mathieu said over the communications network, clapping.

C.C. said, "Commander Musgrove, the mission is yours."

"Thank you, Commander Crenshaw. Crew, prepare for EDL."

"Let's rock 'n' roll," Anna said. "I want to get off this ship. It's time to see some wide open spaces."

"At least as much as you can from inside a DSMU," Mathieu said.

"I'll take it."

Emily pulled up her crew's vitals. Everybody looked good except her husband, whose heart rate was elevated. "Cole, I need you to breath slow and deep. Your vitals are too high."

"I guess I'm nervous. I've never jumped from orbit before."

"Neither have any of us."

"Technically, I have," Mathieu said.

"Except Mathieu," Emily said. "Mathieu's done it all. He could probably do this all without any of us, but NASA won't let him work alone."

"She's right, you know. I met with Director Craft about it. He said NASA policy hasn't caught up with me yet. Cole, let me give you some advice. The trick is to not throw up on the way down, hey. Because if you do, your vomit will first hit the ceiling, but then eventually gravity will suck it right back down onto your face."

"Not helping," Cole said.

"Come on, Cole," Anna said. "It's ten minutes of the best thrill ride ever invented. Think of it like being on a roller coaster dreamed up by the best minds on earth. It is perfectly safe."

"So long as all one hundred pyrotechnics go off according to plan and nobody was sleeping on the job when they installed them," C.C. said. "Also, there are the five hundred thousand lines of code that—fingers crossed—all work and haven't been affected by radiation."

"Those codes have been checked and double-checked by JPL," Emily interjected. "Not to mention, we have radiation recovery protocols in place."

"Don't forget, it's all built by the lowest bidder," C.C. added.

"Really not helping, C.C.," Cole said.

"I don't want to make you nervous, Cole, but there's basically a zero percent margin of error or we die," Mathieu said.

"Mathieu, do you want to stay on this ship while the rest of us explore a world never before visited by mankind?" Emily barked. "Zip it. Cole, your blood pressure is elevated. I cannot start the EDL sequences until your blood pressure has gone down. So I need you to find a happy place. Use the words the brain trust at JSC gave you. The rest of you, I appreciate you taking the chance to get back at my husband's humor, God knows I've wanted a little vengeance there myself. But you've had your fun. Enough."

"Mellifluous," Cole said to himself. He thought of the DSMU frame at a station at the JPL, hung up on a giant crane in the Robot Assembly Building along with the other twelve DSMUs. Contractors wearing clean suits installed the wiring harnesses, the radio assemblies, and weeks later, the carapace. They would bolt the DSMUs to their heat shields. Hell, they would glue the tiles to the heat shield. He hoped they installed everything probably. He hoped they were clearheaded. He hoped that if they saw something wrong during the installation process, they reported it. He hoped that the testing was as thorough as possible and that all the bugs were discovered. It was a lot of hope, but he trusted them.

With your life, his inner monologue reminded him.

Cole stuck the photo of his family between the screens. There was him, Emily, and his sister Clara, who was holding a newborn child. Cole focused while a tear ran down his cheek. "Calm, balanced, serene. Mathieu, C.C., and Anna can go fuck themselves. Mellifluous."

Emily watched her husband's heartbeat lower from 149 bpm to 118 bpm.

"Much better, my love," Emily said. In her EDLS, she toggled away from the abort menu that she had pulled up while everyone was razzing her husband. She moved to the sequence menu. "JEVS, you ready?"

"Yes, ma'am."

"DSMU 1 go for EDL." She punched a button.

The others sounded off.

"DSMU 2 go for EDL."

"DSMU 3 go for EDL."

"DSMU 4 go for EDL."

Emily waited a second. "Cole?"

"Mellifluous," he said. She could hear his slow inhalation over the com, then, "DSMU 5 go for EDL."

Emily said, "JEVS, initiate EDL sequence in 3...2..."

"Mellifluous," Cole said, looking at his family. On his screen Distance from Ground read as 177 kilometers.

"Oh, shit."

There was a loud *boom* and the floor fell out from under his EDLS. Cole was in gravitational freefall.

2

The group of school children sat quietly in the large theater auditorium. Normally, they would be picking their noses and squirming in their seats, but not that day. That day they were visiting an astronaut at the Johnson Space Center in Houston. The astronaut had their full attention.

Dr. Emily Musgrove, who was introduced as the commander of Exo-Planetary Space Expedition (EPSP) 18, stood in a sky blue jumpsuit on a narrow stage above her rapt audience. Behind her, on the giant screen, was that universally revered symbol of space exploration, the NASA logo. A blue circle of the cosmos with the agency's name orbited by some unknown space vehicle—perhaps it was John Glenn in the *Friendship 7*. The acronym "NASA" floated weightlessly among the stars and in between the lines of a bright red chevron, a tip of the hat to the aeronautic purpose behind the agency.

The crowd of children had just finished watching a short video showing kids building all kinds of things using toys, including toy robot build kits, popular world-creation games, and even the old stalwart,

Legos. In the video, the toys were always being used to build science fiction playsets or toy space vehicles.

"Do you like the toys you get to play with?" Emily asked the room.

"Yes!" the enthusiastic crowd shouted back at her.

"Well, these are the toys I get to play with, and these are the things I get to build."

The NASA logo faded, and the agency-created sizzle reel started with old, historical footage of the Mercury and Gemini capsules and NASA's early missions. The children *oohed* at the large booming thunder of Saturn rockets blasting off from Cape Canaveral. They *awwed* at the footage of a space shuttle landing at Kennedy air strip. They got silent as they watched space stations hurtling over the Earth and cheered with the first rockets to Mars. In less than two minutes, the entire history of NASA was provided to them in a historical perspective of space hardware: landers, robots, rovers, submarines, drones, and super drones. The footage video culminated in views of elegant interstellar vehicles and finally, the giant robotic mechs. Kids stood up to get a better view of the mechs. Emily smiled from the stage.

As the video ended and the screen faded to black, a spotlight fell on Emily. "NASA is about exploration. But it is also about perspective." She pressed the button on her clicker, and a life-size model of a Crawler appeared on the screen. The Crawler was too wide to fit on the screen.

"This is a Crawler. It sits over two stories tall. Similar versions of the Crawler were used to move rockets over a hundred years ago." As she spoke, the Crawler shrunk so that it could fit on the screen. The bottom of a rocket appeared to stand on top of the Crawler.

"This is a Delta heavy rocket, which was the rocket that helped us get to Mars."

The Delta shrunk so that it could fit onto the screen. Now the Crawler, which seconds ago was too large for the giant screen, was no more than a small wedge at the bottom.

"Now we have a better rocket, an Omega. These are the workhorses of the Exo-Planet Search Program, the EPSP. Like with your toys where you sometimes have to build one part of the set, then connect it to another part of the set, the Omegas deliver large payloads into low earth orbit, where robots and astronauts at Space Station Hephaestus assemble the interstellar vehicles."

Behind her, thick pieces of thrusters and drives and capsules were launched into the Earth's atmosphere, where they were assembled into a large white and black space ship that made the Omegas look like two-door economy-sized cars parked next to eighteen wheelers.

"Pretty big difference, right?" As the children nodded, she said, "This is IV-104, the Anchor. And it is the best and latest interstellar vehicle built by Titan Space and NASA. But that is only one part of the story. Because we now have to take this giant spaceship, which is bigger and more powerful than anything NASA has ever built, and we have to fling it through space to a faraway planet."

Up on the screen, the giant interstellar vehicle squeezed down next to the Earth, and then a red line shot out from the Earth, past the orbits of Mars and Jupiter and Saturn and then Neptune. With each passing planetary body, the speed of the red line picked up. Within seconds it had passed the Oort cloud and broken free of the solar system.

The cloud joined the shrinking rings of the solar system's planetary orbits, and suddenly stars began to pass at dizzying speeds.

"We have now traveled farther than anyone has ever traveled in the history of humankind," Emily said.

Finally the red line settled on a small system with five orbital rings. The orbital rings grew and grew until large terrestrial bodies floated past the screen and out over the audience.

As the projection moved over the students, a small planet covered in oceans of sand and islands of lakes appeared. "This is 51 Golgotha a, our final destination on our long voyage from Earth. We have traveled 7 light years at this point. We have arrived at a planet that caught our interest because it has something no other exo-planet has yet shown: signs of civilization."

The camera angle swept over the exo-planet's many deserts and came to a jungle. Along the horizon, a tall, gray wall appeared. From behind the wall peeked the tops of twelve long pyramids. They rose slow and steady over the wall, like giant sentinels.

"This is what we have been chasing since before Neil Armstrong walked on the moon. We know we are not alone in the universe. Microbes and fungi have been discovered on other planets. 51 Golgotha has plants. But these pyramids are something totally different. They hold the answers to questions we've been asking since we first looked up at the stars thousands of years ago. Are we the only civilization in the universe?"

The video did not show the fields of dead, mummified bodies that lay beyond the wall. Some things were not meant for school field trips. She was certain the children had seen photos of the aliens. Who hadn't? They were aliens. But this was a government program, not a *Ripley's Believe It Or Not*.

She paused. "But that's not what you came to see, is it?"

7

Kids gasped. On the screen, the point of view of the camera swarmed from the planet back to IV-104 in orbit. The point of view breached the hull of the Anchor. Inside, small robots no bigger than a soccer ball whisked around the ship's interior, performing maintenance chores. They whizzed by larger, bipedal robots that walked heavily down the interstellar vehicle's halls.

"There are robots like these already on 51 Golgotha, taking measurements and relaying data back to us. But not until humans get there will there be robots like these…"

One of the bipedal robots seemed to walk across the screen. It bumped into a shadow, then stepped back as if it had run into something solid in the dark. Out of the shadow emerged the giant robot, a large DSMU, a Dynamic Supplemental Mobility Unit. It was 8 meters tall. The DSMU was painted white and black like a space shuttle, and it had the EPSP 18 mission patch painted on one shoulder and an American flag and NASA logo on the other. Its large feet stepped forward onto the stage. Each step made a big *whumph* noise as the weight of the DSMU met the stage. Only then did the children realize that while they had been looking at the holographic projections above them, the screen had been lifted. An actual DSMU stood on the stage with them. It was so tall it had to duck to fit into the theater. The DSMU raised its arms wide. Its giant robotic arms fanned over the children. Much like theater goers being mesmerized by a chained King Kong, some children smiled, others laughed, and others screamed in glee. And fear.

Then they all cheered and clapped. Even the teachers stood in awe.

Emily looked off stage to her husband Cole, who was sitting on the front row alongside a Public Affairs Office specialist and the JSC Center Director. Emily winked to her husband. Then to the children she said, "Okay, who wants to see the DSMU jump?"

More cheers.

3

Sensors were blaring, most of them warning codes, and none of them serious. The system was not happy with the freefall event. Through the portal window above him, Cole could see the Anchor. It seemed to be falling away from him into space (or maybe he was launching away from it—being in space had really messed with his sense of up and down). He turned to look outside the EDLS. 51 Golgotha was getting closer with every second. It was lush and green and full of alien plants. Anna had been gushing about them the entire course of the trip. He had seen holograms from the autonomous devices already exploring the planet. But now they were actually going there.

Boom! Boom! Boom! Boom! Boom! Boom! Boom! Boom!

Imagine the loudest explosions you have ever heard. These were louder. The sound was so intense, Cole could feel the vibrations rattling in his chest and tickling his ribs. They startled the hell out of him.

The explosions came to a crescendo, and then the shell flew off of the DSMU. The robot lay kneeling in its EDL configuration tethered to the heat shield. An intense orange and red glow was burning all around Cole's DSMU. He was sure that, from an outside perspective, this looked very much like a giant robot skateboarding through the atmosphere. In the future, assuming he survived the landing, he would assure anyone who asked that it was nothing but terrifying.

The world was coming up to meet him as he plummeted to the ground at nine Gs. The status screen showed Environmental Controls and Life Support Systems (ECLSS) as nominal. His kph was somewhere around 500. He was 80 kilometers from ground. As his vision tunneled, he focused on the DSMU temperature readout, which was pushing toward peak heat, 1600 degrees Fahrenheit. And then Cole blacked out.

4

The elevator opened, and Cole walked onto the ninth floor of JSC's Building 1. On the other side of a glass door, the executive admin smiled and waved him on.

"They're waiting for you, hon," she said cheerily.

Suddenly nervous, he checked his watch. "Am I late?"

"Oh, no. You're fine."

The admin opened the door for Cole. Inside the executive suite sat the Center Director (and former astronaut) Dr. Elaine Ybarra. Across from her, stretched out casually, was Dr. Robert Albright, also a former astronaut. Next to him sat Colonel Mitch Brown, the first black man to walk on an exo-planet. He was now the center's "Chief Astronaut" and in charge of running JSC's astronaut corps. In fact, Cole reasoned, he was the only non-astronaut, former or otherwise, in the room. Seated at the table were three people he knew very well, and his wife.

"Hello, Dr. Ybarra," Cole said. He shook her hand.

"Come on in, Cole. You know Robert, Mitch." He shook their hands.

"And of course, Expedition 18," she said. "Dr. Anna Altieri, the medical doctor from Ciudad Juarez; Anchor Commander C.C. Crenshaw; Dr. Mathieu Du Pleises, the EVA specialist and general technology wizard from Paarl, South Africa; C.C. Crenshaw, the geologist from Amarillo; and your wife, planetary commander, also from Amarillo."

"What can I do for you all?"

"Well, first off, I wanted to thank you for everything you've done for us," Dr. Ybarra said. "For three years now you've been working with the mission team to help teach them the language of the Jedik-ikik."

"I can't take all the credit. Dr. Butler and a whole team of linguists deciphered the language and taught it to the crew."

Cole could've sworn he heard Anna giggle under her breath. He started to glance at her to see what was going on, but then Dr. Ybarra said, "Yes. Leo is a fine linguist. One of the smartest in the world. But after the accident, well, it is going to take at least a year for him to fully recover, if he recovers, and we have a timeline."

"I don't understand."

"It's time for you to lose the green stripe, Cole," C.C. said. "You're now a civil servant."

"What?"

Dr. Ybarra gave C.C. a sideways glance. "What he means is, three years ago we asked you to apply to the Astronaut Corps."

"Right. I was turned down."

"You were pulled from the pool of applicants because the government believed you were more useful teaching astronauts. Things have changed. Welcome to Expedition 18, Dr. Musgrove."

Behind him, the four other members of Expedition 18 cheered and clapped.

"Really?" he asked his wife.

"Yeah. Originally it was just going to be me in the room, but I didn't want you to think I pulled rank."

"Screw that," Mathieu said. "We all pulled rank. They asked us. You were the only one on the list."

Cole smiled. "Thanks, guys. I'll try to live up to everything you expected of Leo."

C.C. said out of the side of his mouth, "Oh, now the hard part begins."

5

Cole came to and said, "Oh my God. We're still falling?" He checked his distance. Twenty five kilometers from ground.

What woke him from his blackout was the popping of the parachute. The supersonic chute was made of special materials that could reduce the speed from 500 kph to 300 kph in less than a minute. He checked the heat. It was down to about 1000 degrees Fahrenheit, which meant that—

Wham! The heat shield ejected away from the DSMU. The shield would eventually land sixteen kilometers away, scarring the planet with its collision.

"Mellifluous," Cole said. "The worst part is over. Most of the pyros have been blown, and the heat shield is gone."

Then the warning light blared. Cole's DSMU was coming in too fast. He should have already slowed down to 300 kph already, but he was only at about 350. It was a small discrepancy, but a disastrous one. This meant that—

RIIIIIP!

Cole looked up to the last thing an astronaut wants to see during descent. His chute had outlived its testing. He manually released the chute. Twin ribbons of shiny fabric curled up and away from him. Another set of pops followed, and three smaller drones deployed.

He watched in terror as his computer relayed data to the ground, tracking the landing site, and came to the conclusion that the DSMU would not survive the crash. He tried to suppress the initial pangs of panic and engage his training, which had included parachute fails.

"I can parachute out," Cole said. "Eject to safety."

Wham! Something large and bulky slammed into his DSMU. The world spun as if on an invisible axis.

"That never happened in training!"

Emily's voice came through his com. "Belay eject. Your fall is too fast."

"What do I do?"

"Don't worry. I got you." Out his side window, he could see that Emily's DSMU was in full mech mode, the one the kids loved. She was attached tighter than a tick to his DSMU.

"You've got me? But who's got you?"

"I released my chute when I saw you weren't with us. I tried hailing you, but you didn't answer."

"I'm sorry, baby. I think I blacked out."

"Don't be. I've got an idea. I'm going to do a powered descent with the ascent boosters. It's going to be badass."

The ground was coming up very quickly, and he was feeling sick to his stomach from all the spinning. 183 meters. "Do whatever you have to do."

He heard her set off the ascent rockets. The burning of the boosters crackled outside his DSMU. Alarm bells went off again. The structure of his mech was breaking down due to the heat. The most intense heat was of course close to his own boosters.

"Um, hon…"

"I know. We're almost down. Brace for impact!"

"What does that even mean?"

And then he heard the cracking of tree limbs followed by the crunching of metal and dirt. The DSMU was rolling on the ground, having slammed through the trees like a bowling ball, and he was spinning inside the cockpit. After the hurricane in his head stopped, Cole looked around. He couldn't find his wife, so he shouted for her.

"Emily!" If anything had happened to her...

"I'm okay," she said. They both caught their breath, then Emily added: "This chair works amazingly well."

Cole turned off the EDL and put his DSMU into transport mode. The DSMU determined up from down. Then arms and legs of the DSMU pushed outward from its central cockpit area. The canopy popped open, and Cole dropped out with all the grace of a newborn hippo.

Cole steadied himself, then stood and looked up at 20-meter-tall palm trees. A large debris trail showed his crash landing. On the other end of the trail stood Emily and the other astronauts.

Cole was finally, happily, on the ground.

CHAPTER TWO: LAND OF THE DEAD

1

Three kids in overalls and t-shirts walked through an alien landscape. They were flatlanders, not used to the steep walls of Palo Duro Canyon. For them to see a natural formation higher than a gopher's head was extraordinary. So the walls, which were clearly seven meters of sheer rock and sand, seemed daunting if not impossible. But not to all of them.

"C'mon, Chris. Let's go check it out," Emily said. She punched him in the shoulder to encourage him to go with her and Brian. But Chris was a shy kid, slow to make decisions, and he kept to himself. He was only out here, if he was being honest, because his parents dragged him all the way up from Lubbock to Amarillo.

"I don't know. Are there any handholds or footholds in those rocks?"

"Maybe. If there aren't, what is the problem? Think about it. We could be the first people to climb these rocks."

Brian piped in, scholarly and aloof as a German Shepherd. "I don't know, Emily. This area was populated by a lot of tribes, and after the tribes were kicked out, Charles Goodnight used the area as a resting place on his cattle drives before eventually buying out the whole place. Not to mention all the outlaws who favored it as a hideout."

Instead of glazing over, Emily's pupils dazzled with possibilities. "Ooh. Think about it. We could be walking in the footsteps of outlaws. Maybe they climbed that rock up there so they could get the one-over on some Texas Rangers who were following them."

"I seriously doubt that," Brian said.

"What if we stayed down here and appreciated it from a distance?" Chris asked.

"Where's the fun in that?" Emily shot back. "Unless you're chicken."

"Hey, you stop that!"

13

"Chicken Chris! Chicken Chris!" Emily taunted. As Chris ran up to tackle her, she nimbly jumped upward from rock to rock and scampered out of reach.

"C'mon," she said. "This is easy. You won't get hurt. I promise." She crawled back down the red rock and extended a hand to Chris. He looked at it for a second as if making some grand decision, and then he took it. She helped pull him up onto a small ledge of clay and sand. "Put your foot between the two rocks there. That's it. Now you're rocking. Get it? Rocking?"

"You are not as amusing as you think you are," Brian said. He grabbed a handhold in the rock and followed Chris and Emily up the stone face.

The rock face was tough to climb because of how steeply it weaved back and forth through red and white striations. Chris felt like if he leaned back too far, he'd topple all the way down and break his crown like Jack and Jill.

"I know it seems scary, but everything that's hard seems scary at first." Her footing slipped on a sandy embankment. She grabbed the gypsum rocks to catch herself, then kicked a foothold into the sand. "It never seems scary after you've done it."

Chris turned around and looked at the steep canyonside. He felt dizzy. He hunched down, nearly losing his footing, and screamed. "I want to go back down," he said.

"You can't go back now," Emily said. "You're almost to the top. If you turn around now, you'll only regret it."

Chris got real quiet. Brian, standing beneath Chris, scrunched up his nose with frustration.

"If it makes you feel better," Brian said, "Emily is probably wrong. Did you see the line of cars at the entrance to the park? So many people vacation here that, statistically speaking, we are probably not even the first thousand park visitors to climb this canyon wall. Look over there." He pointed to a shoeprint. "See that? Others have been here."

"That's Emily's," Chris said.

"Nuh-uh," she called back. "I promise. Come on, Chris. You can do this. I believe in you."

Chris took a deep breath, then he took another handhold.

Evening was setting by the time the three reached the top. The canyon was bathed in golden sunlight. Pink and purple clouds puckered in the blue sky. The canyon walls seemed to be on fire, they were so vibrantly red.

"See?" Emily said. "Isn't it beautiful?" Her tone changed when she asked her friends about the beauty of the sunset. She was more wistful. "I could stay up here all night."

Chris said, "Okay, this was fun. I'm ready to go now. How do I get down?"

"Oh, Chris." Emily wrapped her arms around both her friends. "Just enjoy this moment. This is how you start exploring."

2

"This isn't how you start exploring," Cole said, looking around at the broken and dented parts of the DSMUs.

The low gravity of 51 Golgotha made for very tall trees and even taller mountains, as if some god-like being had pulled on the branches and peaks to lengthen them. The branches twisted and wrapped around the trunks of other trees to the point where it was hard to see where one tree ended and the other started. Their roots, too, maneuvered around rocks to get to thin layers of sand and soil. To Cole, it seemed as if the floor was made of snakes.

C.C., Anna, and Mathieu came to them from their landing site a hundred meters away. They had landed hand-in-hand, which was the plan for all five to reach the planet at the same time, until Cole's DSMU ran into trouble.

The five astronauts worked on determining what repairs, if any, needed to be done to the DSMUs. C.C.'s DSMU had sustained minor structural damage from his landing. Emily's had booster wiring that had come unloose and needed to be reconnected.

"So this is how we start the historical exploration of a new alien planet: with repairs," Cole said.

Anna agreed. "Cole's right. I want to go exploring. Get a look at these plants and start collecting them."

"Simmer down, Anna. You'll get your chance," Emily said. "We have protocols to follow."

First, Emily called in to the Anchor to relay a message to Mission Data Collection in Houston, a message explaining their situation, which was that the landing did not go as well as hoped and two of the DSMUs were damaged, and another lost 25% of its ascent fuel.

The message was purely ceremonial at this point. They had long ago stopped having two-way communication with Houston. A weird fact was that according to plan, they would arrive back on Earth before most of their messages returned. The only reason to send them was as a redundancy, should something catastrophic happen to the team. For all intention, they were completely isolated from human civilization, and had been for most of the past seven years of flight.

JEVS, which operated as their mission control, said, "My survey data shows your landing approximately five kilometers from the Habitation Module. Is this correct, sir?"

"Yes, JEVS," Emily said.

"What do you think, Mathieu?" Emily asked.

Mathieu was kneeled down at an open console, his laptop connected to the DSMU. "Most of the damage is superficial. Cracks and warped shielding. And since the armor is matrixed to the Hab for maximum redundancy, we can cannibalize some of them if we really want to. I'm more concerned with the left leg's secondary piston. It was damaged in the landing. He'll still be able to walk, so again, nothing catastrophic. Once we get back to the Hab, I can fix this. It'll be fun."

"There is a spare DSMU ready to deploy if necessary," JEVS relayed to them from the Anchor.

"Thank you, but I think we are fine for now. If DSMU 5's mobility is compromised, we will talk then."

"Before we leave," C.C. said, "we need to take the photo. This is a historic moment."

Each DSMU was outfitted with a leg camera for just this reason. They stood arms together for the group shot.

"Say 'cheese,'" JEVS said.

"Screw that," Cole said. "Everybody say 'We made it!'"

The faces weren't all clear, but the joy was in the arms no longer together, but raised in celebration. A second photo was taken with the interlocking arms, as was decided years ago when the mission was first conceived. Picture taken, C.C. said, "Send to Titan Space for public dissemination."

"Now, let's go find our new home," Emily said. They climbed back into their DSMUs and began the long march to the Hab module.

3

There are few things more important to NASA than medical analysis. All medical analyses are used to better understand the effects of spaceflight on an astronaut's health, which in turns teaches NASA how to improve the survivability of future missions. To that end, it can be said that NASA's priorities are 1. Survive, and 2. Document that survival through medical testing.

So while Day 1 was spent adjusting to life on a terrestrial planet, the astronauts also spent the day peeing in cups and giving seemingly endless bottles of blood. Then there were the breathing tests and peripheral vision tests and balance tests and psychological programs to evaluate their mental flexibility. On the plus side, the astronauts had little in the way of down time, which was a boon because with too much time on their hands, they would get the urge to jump out of the Hab and go explore the Golgothan terrain.

Three of the astronauts stood at the long window, enjoying the view of 51 Golgotha. They wore suits designed to assist the body's re-accommodation to a full gravitational environment, even if the gravity of 51 Golgotha was roughly equivalent to the gravity of Mars, which was about a third of Earth's gravity, and also was the gravity setting of the Anchor's living quarters.

Close to the Hab, the OGRA (Operational GRound Assist) robots worked at repairing the DSMUs and transitioning supplies from the DSMU storage holds to the habitation module. Emily noticed that, like some of the crewmembers' uniforms, the OGRA robots had the "Titan Space" logo, a large, blue letter T with a yellow bolt of lightning across it.

"When do we get to go out there?" C.C. asked as he stepped away from a bipedal OGRA robot. OGRA had been collecting blood for bone loss studies.

"Mission protocol," Emily responded. She sipped her green tea while she continued typing her log entry. "The requirement is at least 24 hours to acclimate to 51 Golgotha. Plus, medical testing has to be completed."

In the distance, the steep Calvary Mountains rose over the jungle canopy. On the other side of those mountains lay the pyramids, and the alien civilization.

"I just want to be there already," C.C. said. "Doesn't anybody else feel the same way? Today, we could be putting our hands on an alien civilization's empire instead of being cooped up here all day like a bunch of kids in time-out."

"Patience," Emily said. "Space travel is hard on the body, and OGRA and JEVS need to verify that all of us are mission ready before we can conduct any operations. If you're eager to move around, there is plenty of low-impact cardio tests to conduct."

"If we had a health problem, they'd have found it by now. We were chosen in part because our bodies are so unbreakable. I was an Army Ranger. Anna, an Olympian. We're good. We can go."

"According to NASA's Human Research Program, there are over 1000 ways for you to die because of interstellar travel."

"Don't be like that."

"And some of those are just risks, not necessarily 'kill you immediately' problems, but risks, like pancreatic malfunction, kidney stones, renal stones, vertebra damage, brain damage, ocular damage that could cause blindness, inner ear problems so you lose your balance. Your gut and intestinal bacteria could be ravaged, you could develop osteoporosis, your heart could get arrhythmia. The little ends on your chromosomes could be damaged. Need I go on?"

"Come on, Em," C.C. said. "Don't tell me you don't want to be out there. Not you."

"I do want to be there, C.C., but let's not get jumpy. I want to survive the encounter. That means our bodies need to rest and adjust. There will be plenty of time for exploring later. In the meantime…"

She slid an electronic medical questionnaire across the table screen to C.C. "You've got questionnaires to fill out."

C.C. filled out the first half, then said, "Can I talk to you in private, commander to commander?"

"Sure."

C.C. walked her back to his private bunk. He tried shutting the door. Emily stuck her arm out. From the corner of her eye, she saw Cole watching them, his face flush with concern, and maybe jealousy, too.

The bunk rooms were no penthouse suites. There was barely enough room for a bed. Emily was so close to C.C. she could see the scar on his chin that he got from their travails in Palo Duro. It was no more than a ghost of a scar now, so many years later, but it was as real to her now as it was when he first got it.

Under his breath, C.C. said, "There was a time you'd be the first one running out the door, Em. Leading me and Brian up the side of Palo Duro and down into some playa lake. What happened to you? Do I need to dare you to jump off a rock?"

"The only thing you need to do is drink plenty of fluids and keep your strength up, C.C. We'll get to Ximortikrim soon enough, and we'll have plenty of time for you to jump off as many rocks as you like. But until then, don't get cabin fever on me. And get your task list done."

Emily returned to Cole and Anna in the main room. She caught Anna saying, "Neil Armstrong and Buzz Aldrin had to wait 6 hours before taking their first steps on the moon. We can wait a day."

Cole reached for Emily's hand. "You okay?"

She nodded. "Fine." She looked around. Something had seemed off, and now she could place it. She opened the door to the exercise and testing room, then the bathroom. She turned to Anna and Cole. "Where's Mathieu?"

The two astronauts glanced around. "I thought he was in his room," Cole muttered, while crossing the Hab to check. The small room was empty.

"There he is," C.C. said, exiting Mathieu's room and pointing outside.

Mathieu was sitting on a cargo bin next to Cole's broken DSMU. His backpack leaned against the bin. Inside was an emergency kit of pliers, wrenches, and ratchets. Two robots held the leg's outer shell back while he worked on the broken piston. He reached for the torque wrench in his pack, but instead grabbed air. He tried, and failed, a second time. He looked at the robots, but they stood there stoic, without answer or judgement.

Anna pressed the com button on the wall. "You good, Mathieu?"

"Everything's sharp sharp."

He wasn't going to miss again, especially with the doctor watching. Three misses in front of everyone would mean his hand-eye coordination was suffering from the effects of gravity, so he squinted his eyes and slowly reached for the wrench. His fingers wrapped around the handle. He'd be okay, he assured himself.

Emily pressed the com button on the wall and said, "Mathieu, you need to get back in here You need to rest so that your body can acclimate to the gravity. And I hate to break it to you, too, but everybody seems to be forgetting that they have reports to fill out."

"I'll be done in a minute," he said into his helmet's microphone.

"Mathieu."

"Commander, hey, I couldn't let this beautiful machine go another minute without repair. Sorry for not saying anything. I wanted to get outside. You know, get a little fresh air." He took a deep breath of recycled suit air to light-heartedly emphasize his point.

Anna laughed. As the exo-biologist who'd spent years studying the atmosphere and flora of 51 Golgotha, she knew better than most the dangerous repercussions of the alien planet's highly toxic atmosphere. At the surface, 51 Golgotha had very little breathable air, but plenty of carbon monoxide. Sure, the first few breaths would feel alright. Your head wouldn't explode and your lungs wouldn't turn to fire. But after a few deep breaths, any human not wearing a life support system would start getting a bad headache. That headache would worsen by the second. Within a minute, they'd be coughing violently as their lungs tried to get rid of all the excess carbon monoxide. If they were outside of their AXES suit, they'd be asleep inside of five minutes. They'd be dead within ten.

4

The five astronauts sat at a circular table in a simple, low-lit room in the Astronaut Beach House at Kennedy Space Center. For such a simple room, it held a lot of history. The first astronauts to leave Earth's atmosphere had stayed in this same cottage along the Atlantic Coast. So had members of Challenger and Columbia and Crockett.

The view, though, was nothing short of spectacular. The eastern windows would waken the astronauts. The sun rising out of the Atlantic would be the last sunrise they would see for many years.

The western side was just as brilliant. Florida blessed the astronauts with a wide sunset splashed with fading purples, brilliant yellows, and red the color of dying embers. The vista was punctuated by Pads 40 and 41. Their Sigma Six Rocket stood on the pad, waiting for the crew to launch into their destiny.

Lift-off was scheduled for the next morning at 1000 hours EST. The past five days they had received visitors from politicians and NASA administration, as well as family and friends. Always from a distance, though. While exo-planet missions were long duration, and the chances of sickness almost certain, NASA still required healthy astronauts on liftoff, and they had placed a lot of funding and time into ensuring the health of the astronauts. From 90 days out, testing started. The astronauts' healths were assessed and reassessed as they got closer to lift-off. Blood, urine, spit, hair follicles, cheek swabs. Everything was collected to develop that all-important medical baseline before they stepped foot in a space ship.

Despite the advances in technology, liftoff was still the most dangerous part of the mission. Should anything happen on the six-minute voyage to low earth orbit, NASA needed quick-thinking astronauts to make instantaneous decisions. There was no time for fuzzy-headed men and women with runny noses.

That morning, each crewmember had been given enemas. It was still a two-day trip to Space Station Hephaestus with nothing more than diapers to take care of evacuations.

But tradition was tradition, and the astronauts had their last meal that night—an uninspired menu of water and oatmeal.

Cole spooned his oatmeal and let it plop back down in his bowl. "This is our last meal on Earth?"

C.C. said, "Well, we didn't come here for the food, did we?"

Anna smiled. "Historically, barbecues were really popular the night before. But that was a long time ago. Now, you could've chosen steak and baked potato if you wanted, Cole…and crap your diaper on the way up to Hephaestus."

They all laughed.

Emily said, "Listen, before we go up there, C.C. and I wanted to say that training with you three has been the pleasure of our careers. It is so odd saying goodbye to our parents and siblings and nieces and nephews and cousins. We all know the risks, and we all know that some of these people could be gone to us, and we wouldn't be able to do anything about it. We probably wouldn't know about it for twelve years. But I am comforted by the knowledge that I've gained a family in all of you."

Anna wiped a tear from her eye. Everyone looked to C.C. with at least a little mistiness.

"I am not as inspiring as Emily. I blame it on my military background. I was eight years old when this kid in jeans with rips in the knees convinced me to climb rocks in Palo Duro Canyon. I was 26 when I found out she'd joined NASA as an astronaut, and when I was 28 I discovered we'd both be commanding the first human landing on 51 Golgotha a. Mathieu was in my astronaut selection class, and we quickly became great friends who enjoyed feuding over barbecue and beer. Anna I met, strangely enough, doing PR at Comic-Con. Only one of you I don't like—Cole," he said with a smile, "but the rest of you I can tolerate. Seriously, I can oscillate between a heartless taskmaster and the guy who just wants to get to the mountain summit first. You all remember how I was in Colorado. NASA calls me a commander, but I feel it is you who lifts me up."

He raised his glass of water. "May the next meal on land be better than this one."

5

That night, the crew ate their first meal on another planet. As tradition dictated, the meal was spaghetti. The tomatoes for the sauce had been grown in the greenhouse months before their arrival. When Anna discovered there was no oregano manifested, she threatened to cancel the whole mission until she got some. The favorite, though, was the meatballs. Fresh ground beef rolled up into little balls. It was the first fresh meat they'd had in years that hadn't been synthesized protein. C.C. and Anna's plates, in particular, were mostly meatballs with a few noodles thrown in for good measure.

While the others laughed at Anna's pretend threat, Cole sat in a corner looking at photographs of the ancient civilization's hieroglyphs and practicing his language skills.

"Dee tlick-ikik. Mopneefrrrik."

Emily came over with a plate of spaghetti. "I made it heavy on the marinara, just as you like."

The spaghetti smelled delicious. Even though the meals on the Anchor were as good as anything he'd ever had, there was something about printed food he struggled with. The texture was always a little off.

Also, all foods were fortified with iodine, vitamin E, and several other radiation-resistant chemicals that the astronauts had to take at every meal. Of course, they'd all gotten used to the taste. Still, the heaping pile of noodles and marinara in his wife's hands smelled like everything that was right about food.

He pecked her on the cheek and thanked her for the food, quickly clearing a spot among his binders and tablets.

"Sreenap," he said in thanks.

"Is he speaking in bug again?" Mathieu asked from the eating table. "Cole, say something in bug. Say 'C.C. is a tool.'"

"Don't be crass. You know better. They aren't 'bugs.' They're Jedik-ikik."

"Homo-insectus," Emily added. She pulled up a photo on one of his tablets and expanded it on their wall. The photo showed the dusty remains of a man with two legs, four arms, and mandibles instead of jaws.

"Second," Cole continued. "I don't know their equivalence for 'tool,' at least as you mean it, which is more like 'douchebag.' I don't know how to say that."

"Well, say something cool."

He thought for a second. "Mathieu p'rok l'tik berrrininimi zree, zree berrrininimi p'rockiz."

"Wow. That sounds really weird. What'd you say?"

Cole had a big smile on his face. "I've been teaching you this language for more than half a decade. You should be fluent in it by now. You tell me what I said."

"I think he cussed you out, Mathieu," C.C. said.

"No way. I made sure to learn the curse words. C'mon, Cole. What'd you say?"

"I think if you spent more time learning grammar and less time studying vulgarities, you wouldn't have this problem, Mathieu."

The crew laughed while Cole crossed to his room. "Good night, everyone. Big day, tomorrow!"

"Big day for you!" Mathieu hollered back. "All we had to do was get you here." He looked at Anna and Emily and C.C., who had all gone silent.

"Give it a rest," Mathieu said. They laughed harder.

"Hang on, Cole. Get back in here," C.C. said.

Cole walked back into the main room.

"So, for posterity's sake and for all the cameras positioned around us," C.C. said, twirling his finger to the cameras in the room. Every room had at least three cameras, and the main Hab room had twenty.

"Tell me what you are thinking on the eve of this historic expedition, Dr. Musgrove."

To nobody's surprise, he said, "I've got a lot of nervous energy, C.C." With less levity, he then said, "It's totally unprecedented, participating in an expedition like this. And I don't just mean that from a space exploration standpoint. What I mean is, in terms of human archaeology, usually we know almost nothing of the civilization before we enter its tombs. All we have are ghost stories and regional folklore warning us to beware entering the tomb or else suffer the curse, that sort of thing. We might have some knowledge of their language based on study of the people who currently live in the vicinity of the ancient temple, but not much else. This time, thanks to robotics, we've already explored a good chunk of Ximortikrim. The catacombs in the pyramids are mapped, as is the layout of all the buildings. We've been able to study the Jedik-ikik and learn about their language, history, and culture from old stone manuscripts. So we'll have a much greater knowledge base when we enter the ancient city. Setting foot into an alien culture, physically and metaphorically? It'll be amazing."

C.C. looked at Anna. "'Amazing?' Can you believe this guy? I ask him to say something nice, and all he comes up with is amazing. Some linguist. What are your thoughts, Anna?"

"One small step for womankind, one giant leap for women."

Emily *wooted* and raised her glass of water.

"And you, Blondie?"

Mathieu said, "Een klein stap vir Suid-Afrikaners…"

"'N reuse-sprong vir alle mense," Cole finished.

"Very good, Cole," Mathieu said.

Cole gave him a thumbs up. "I'll be here all night."

C.C. said, "I'm guessing that was something very poetic in Afrikaans."

Mathieu said, "I'm a techy. Screw poetry. No offense, Cole."

"None taken."

"And you, our fearless commander?" C.C. asked Emily.

"I'm just happy to be here with all of you."

She received a round of *awws*.

Emily added, "But now you, C.C. We've saved the best for last, right?"

"Sure," he said, and then belched.

After the laughter died down, Emily said, "This is it. This is why I live and breathe, and I think you are all very much like me or you wouldn't have sacrificed your lives to be here. You live to explore. To walk where no one else has walked, to find the adventure after the trail ends. This is more than strange planets and alien civilizations. It's about discovering what's out there, and unraveling the possibilities of the universe."

There was silence and nodding. And then another belch.

6

OGRA was scheduled to wake the crew at 0600 hours Local Crew Time. But the opening bars to R.E.M.'s "Stand" found the beds empty and the astronauts gone. As Michael Stipe sang about knowing your direction, the crew was already up and pulling gear and reviewing the daily activities. OGRA turned the song off half-way through. Later, she had to remind the crew to eat breakfast before leaving for the site—fresh eggs, bacon, and brewed coffee thanks to the Animal Station.

Not everything could be trained and practiced down to the minute. That was a change between old NASA Apollo and Space Shuttle missions that lasted days or weeks versus missions spanning decades. But the events could be planned and scheduled.

The team reviewed the Daily Activities List for their second day on 51 Golgotha a. Everything with specific time requirements was written in red: Depart in the DSMUs for Ximortikrim at 0800, arrive at Ximortikrim at 1000. Visit the primary site at 1100, a small pyramid close to the entrance that showed a lot of archaeological promise. Lunch at 1200, followed by a one-hour rest, and then an afternoon touring several other buildings and gravesites. There would be no sample collections of fauna or geology. Day 2 was purely a one-giant-leap moment, fully documented by drones and robots. First dinner at 1600. At 1900 they would depart from Ximortikrim for the Hab module. Second dinner at 2000 hours. Review, communication, and debrief until 2400 hours, when they would go to bed. For people on Earth it was a long time to be awake, but ever since leaving Low Earth Orbit, the crew had been preparing for the planet's 32-hour day. The human performance psychologists at JSC had come up with the new plan, which called for two small dinners as well as a mandatory nap, or "space siesta" as Cole called it.

Of course, this was all Plan A. Plan B toured fewer sites and returned the crew back into the Hab module by 1500 hours. Plan A was based on good adaptation to the planet after years in a spaceship, which is why every crewmember had to pass certain physical and psychological tests that morning before the crew committed to either plan. Plan B was shorter because it embraced the potential realities of returning onto a planet. Emily reminded the crew that Plan B was the more likely scenario, and she would make the call at lunch.

24

Outside, Anna saw C.C. packing a borer and several small sample collection boxes in his DSMU.

"Emily said no collection."

"Emily is NASA. We are Titan Space. And besides, I always come prepared. You never know when an opportunity might arise."

Anna included a few boxes for collecting samples, too. She told herself it was only for things that blew her mind away as so spectacular, she had to analyze it that night in the lab module.

Cole found Emily at the ISRU Station. Getting to 51 Golgotha was only half the problem. The other half was living on a hostile planet and then, years later, being able to leave the hostile planet. Both required energy, and since there wasn't a gas station for a few trillion kilometers, the best thing to do was make their own fuel using the resources available to them. While Anna would've loved to try making her own bio-fuel, NASA had a tried-and-true technology called the In-Situ Resource Utilization Station, which was a fancy term for superheating the dirt until the atoms split into gas atoms like hydrogen and oxygen. The solids were replaced into the ground, and the gas components were stored in giant tanks and pumped into the Ascent Vehicle for fuel.

Cole came up behind Emily and kissed her on the nape of her neck. She shivered and turned on him. "Ooh, you know you shouldn't do that," she said, a smile playing on her lips.

"You ready to go?"

"Sure. I was just—"

"Checking the ISRU Station's metrics, even though you reviewed them from the Anchor yesterday, and the week before yesterday."

"I'm the commander. I need to verify that everything is working as it should."

"You're nervous."

"Being thorough does not equate to nervousness."

"Yeah, but for you, it does. I've seen you walk into a room full of senators and argue why the change of crewmember personnel wouldn't affect the mission timeline."

"Well, I really liked the new crewmember," she said softly, kissing him.

Cole kissed her back, then said, "My point is, twenty minutes before the meeting, you weren't reviewing politician cheat sheets to help you win the argument. You didn't need to review them. You knew everything you needed to know. You only start checking things out at the last minute when something is under your skin. So what's eating you up, buttercup?"

"One, you know I don't like that word. Two, I've got a feeling." She pushed away from him while speaking.

"Oh, no," Cole said with all the weight of *here it comes again.*

"The last time I had a feeling, my trainer crashed. I had to parachute out."

"I know. You scared me half to death."

"And then the other time I had a bad feeling—"

"You don't need to tell me about that one. I know it, you know it, and I don't want to talk about it."

"Okay, okay. We don't have to go there. I was just trying to win the argument."

"Which you always do."

"Not every time. Every once in a while I throw you a bone to make you feel like you're winning."

Cole crossed his arms.

"I just have a feeling, Cole. I want you to do something for me. When we get to Ximortikrim, don't try anything."

"Who? Me?"

"You know what I mean. You are a Nervous Nancy until you get into something, and then you dig into it like a tick, and nobody can get you out."

Cole chuckled. "A tick? Me? Don't worry. I won't be a tick."

"Thank you." But as they walked back to the Hab, Emily couldn't shake her anxiety.

7

By 0730, the eager crew left the Hab module. The distance was too far for the OGRA bipedal robots to follow, so they stayed behind and waved at the monstrous DSMUs stomping off into the jungle mountains. This was the reason NASA chose DSMUs over rovers. Even the sturdiest Jeep rovers lacked the reliability of the DSMUs in crossing the steep mountainous terrain that was covered in thick, cordy vines.

The DSMUs jostled up the side of the first gray-rocked mountain. The course had been plotted before the mission ever left Earth. Very little input was required from the astronauts while the DSMUs moved up and over the mountain.

The low gravity caused for some of the most dramatic mountain peaks they had ever seen. Long barbs, like the spires of giant churches, rose from the top of the mountain. They were a spine along the mountain's backbone. Between the peaks, the crew stopped to survey the area: where they had come and their destination. Across the land, a heavy mist soaked into the jungles.

To the south lay the Hab module, nestled in jungle lowland trees. The tall Ascent Vehicle's upper rocket and crew compartment towered over the jungle canopy. North of them lay the giant wall of Ximortikrim and its twelve pyramids and alien aqueduct system. Only the very tops of the pyramids, wall, and aqueduct appeared. The rest lay submerged in fog.

After taking a moment to take in the view, the astronauts descended out of the mountain pass and back into the jungle.

A few minutes later, Mathieu asked Anna, "Why aren't there any animals? It seems like a jungle would be full of them. It's like something doesn't want them to live."

"There's no evidence that evolution requires animals. Earth's own evolution shows hundreds of millions of years of vegetation without any animals," Anna said.

As if on command, Emily pulled back a curtain of vines. Half-submerged in the rock and vines lay a giant skull, at least the size of a two-story house. The skull appeared almost dinosaurian.

"I swear that looks like a dragon," Anna said. "Look at those horns!"

The drones flying above slowed down to photograph the discovery.

While the others stood in awe, C.C. opened his DSMU and hopped out. "I've got to take a sample." He grabbed his tools, turned on his green-lighting, and began ascending the skull.

"Wait. What are you doing with the sample containment boxes?" Emily asked. "This is supposed to be only a brief tour of the area and the artifacts."

"Looks like it was a good thing I brought the box, Em."

He ascended the skull and broke off a small piece with his borer. Using tweezers, he dropped the shard in the sample containment box and began carbon dating the supply using samples and techniques developed during the initial stages of the planet's discovery.

Anna stepped out of her DSMU, and then the others followed her. Smiling with wonder, she placed her hands on the skull.

"The low gravity meant the creatures could grow to astounding proportions: heights and lengths that our largest animals could only dream of. This gargantuan is easily the largest extinct animal ever discovered. It positively dwarfs any sauropod found on Earth."

"Jislaaik," Mathieu said, staring up at the giant skull.

The others used little bumps and indentations in the skull to climb to the top of its dome where C.C. already stood staring off into the distance. His lights disappeared into the heavy fog. The wall stood before them, immense and foreboding, a measurement of the outsider.

C.C. looked at his wristband. "The results are in. This animal, which I will name 'C.C.-asaurus Rex,' is four thousand years old. Approximately the same age as the ruins."

"So now we know what the wall was for," Mathieu said.

"To keep the C.C.-asaurus out? I don't think so," Anna said.

"A, It's 'C.C.-asaurus Rex,' and B, are you seeing the size of this thing?" C.C. said incredulously.

Anna rolled her eyes. "Ego aside, there's no evidence the wall kept this creature out. On Earth, the largest animals were herbivores and non-threatening. Whatever it kept out was much more dangerous. Right, Cole?"

As resident cultural ambassador to the alien civilization, Cole said, "The assumption has always been warring civilizations. Granted, there is no hard evidence for warring factions. There are six civilization sites on 51 Golgotha, but they are all thousands of kilometers away from each other. I don't think they were constantly engaging in war any more than the American colonies were warring with Polynesian tribes."

"All good conversations," Emily said, "but we have a schedule to keep, and I don't want to get behind. Let's move on."

8

The black granite wall stood thirty meters tall and 6 meters thick at the base. Vines, moss, and lichens had taken up habitation in the walls. Mushrooms and toadstools grew out of several sections of rock.

C.C. put his DSMU in Follow Mode and climbed out of his compartment. He pressed his gloved hand on the wall. The rock was coarse.

"This wall is five times taller than the Great Wall of China," C.C. said. "That makes it the largest wall in the history of civilization."

"Our known history of civilization," Cole corrected. He, too, had climbed out of his DSMU. The others followed suit.

"Right," C.C. said perfunctorily. Then, "Can you imagine what it would have taken to shape, much less move, these rocks? They didn't have bulldozers or carriers or anything, at least that we know. And somehow they built all this."

Anna said, "The Great Wall of China was built for trade routes and foreign invaders, so it had turrets, cannons, and a way to move along the top of the wall. This wall has a few outposts, but nothing as grand as the Great Wall. Do you still think it was built to keep ancient monsters out?"

"Really big monsters, maybe," Mathieu said.

"I'd hate to meet the giant ass creature this wall keeps out," Cole said.

"Just one more mystery to solve. So many opportunities," Anna said. "If I discover why this wall was built, I will put it in a paper, or better yet, my book, and for the rest of eternity, when people talk about this wall, they will talk about the research of Anna Altieri."

"Anna Altieri, the vainglorious," Cole said.

"It's not about fame," Anna said as she approached the gates. "It's about immortality."

"Well, trust me on this," Mathieu said. "We're all getting schools named after us. That goes with the job."

Cole said, "A school? Screw that. I want a porn star to name his move after me. A special move he'd do called 'The Musgrove.'"

"Hey," Emily said. That was all she said, but it was enough. Even Cole understood it was time to shut up and soak in the atmosphere. There would be time for jokes later.

Mathieu finally broke the silence.

"I was wondering if we could take a moment," he said. "This is the first time humans entered an alien civilization. I would like to say the Nicene Creed. You don't have to join me, and if you want, I will join you in yours, but I would like to say it."

Emily nodded. The others stopped and bowed their heads.

"We believe in one God, the Father Almighty, Maker of the Heavens and the Earth, and all that is seen and unseen."

As Anna joined Mathieu in reciting the Nicene Creed, Cole stared at the cypher over the broken gate. The language of the aliens was written like code, with few letters and many accents. The ancient cypher read, "If you need, you will be provided. If you take..." The last part of the cypher had been destroyed.

Cole looked at the civilization beyond the broken gates and into Ximortikrim. The pyramids were there, as were the answers to all their questions, he was sure of it. And humor aside, Mathieu was right. Whether or not they wanted it, this journey would bring them fame like they had never imagined.

Mathieu finished the rite, saying, "We look forward to the resurrection of the dead, and the life of the world to come."

Emily looked at her clock. "We're doing well on time. How is everyone feeling? Does anyone need a break? Does anybody feel weak in the legs or just an overall sense of fatigue? There's no shame in it. That's why the Plan B was developed."

But if anyone felt any kind of fatigue, they weren't admitting it.

9

Inside the walls, it was like the ground was salted or poisoned. Nothing grew. Corpses of Jedik-ikik lay fallen on the ground, strewn about as if stricken down by a sonic cannon.

"Resurrection City," Anna said.

"The reason Titan Space was so eager to participate," C.C. said as he dropped down and collected another sample. This time, Emily did not say anything. C.C. held up the containment box for Anna to see. "The potential answer to life after death."

Emily led the group to their first stop of the grand tour of Ximortikrim: the Small Pyramid.

Like the wall and the other, smaller buildings, the Ximortikrim pyramids were composed of the same black granite. Unlike ancient Egyptian pyramids on Earth, the pyramids of homo-insectus were slim and conical, with one entrance at the bottom and two exits at the top. Early study of the pyramids determined these openings to be wind tunnels to reduce heat and humidity, and not entrances for flying homo-insectus. So far, there was no evidence that homo-insectus could fly or even had wings.

Four statues atop pillars guarded the pyramid. Each one was a little different, which had led many historians to believe that the statues were monuments to specific people. One carried a small half-cane in his hand. Another was stooped and staring at the ground pensively. He was known popularly as the "Squatter." Much conjecture had been given to the spot on the ground where the alien stared because from that point spiraled out the stonework for the rest of the city. The giant spiral rotated outward until its stone path broke like a wave against the city's outer wall. The artistry in each wave was amazing. The waves were perfectly lined up. Even if a line was interrupted by a building, on the far side of the building, the spiral would continue as if the building had been built around it. At the center of the spiral the group took a photo, as the alien statue watched them, half his face broken off due to the wearing of time.

The third statue was the most damaged. Only its feet remained on its pillar. The rest of the stone monument had toppled over. Its wide-spread arms were cracked and segmented. Its head was decapitated by some unseen sword. Luckily, the statue had fallen away from the pyramid.

The fourth statue drew as much interest as the Squatter. The "Pointer," it was christened. A giant granite alien stood out front, one hand raised to the sky, pointing. Much speculation had been made of the statue's purpose. Where was it pointing? Was it pointing at something specific? Dozens of simulations and recreations had failed to answer the question of where it was pointing and why, though people liked to believe hope and a promise of the future had something to do with it.

This pyramid was one of the reasons NASA agreed to the journey. Putting human beings on the ground and looking at the sky from the statue's perspective, many argued, may solve the Puzzle of the Pointer, as it had come to be known.

Standing behind the statue, though, Cole could not see why this statue was so important. Perhaps the Pointer was more interesting to them as outsiders than it had been to the Jedik-ikik? He would have to think on this during the expeditions.

The DSMUs, too tall to enter the pyramid, remained outside in standby mode while the astronauts explored inside.

"And remember," Emily warned them, "We've got one hour in the pyramid, so don't stray, and don't collect." She scowled at Anna and C.C., who tossed up his hands at her.

The first room was an antechamber, large enough for a crowd to gather. Old, rotted paintings adorned the walls. A string of alien hieroglyphs rounded the ceiling.

Mathieu reached out to one of the paintings.

"Don't touch them," Cole said. "These artifacts are so fragile, they'll probably fall apart if you touch them."

The drones, however, filmed as much footage as they wanted.

A stone door lay open on the far side of the room, beckoning. Explorers all, they couldn't resist the invitation.

The second room was long and narrow and dark. On either side stood rows of cabinets holding ancient paper scrolls and stone books. Cole read the small stone insert above the door: the Far-Seeing Room.

Cole saw another inscription. It was written in the wall. He went and gently wiped off the dust and dirt.

"What are you doing?" Emily chastised him.

Cole stood back and pointed. "It is the same phrase as was inscribed on the main gate. 'If you need, you will be provided. If you take—' The rest of the glyph is destroyed."

"What do you make of it?" Anna asked.

"I don't want to jump to conclusions," Cole said. "But guys, I'm starting to think there was a revolution here. All the dead bodies, the toppled statues and the broken glyphs. It's like somebody is trying to wipe out the history of this place."

C.C. squatted down next to the cabinets. He brushed the dust off a wooden cube with stone inlays. The dust motes fluttered in the beams of his headlamps.

"Check this out," he said. He brushed his hand over an insignia of a Jedik-ikik's head. Below the head was a Jedik-ikik skull. He pushed against the head, and the insignia swiveled in a circle and came to a stop. "Does anybody know what to make of it?"

Cole brushed some more dust aside. Shallow hieroglyphs appeared in a circle around the insignia. "These are numbers. I think this is a combination lock. The Jedik-ikik culture is strongly connected to the dichotomies. So a way to say the opposite of something is to say the first thing, then say it backwards. This is like that. Say the first thing, life," and he pointed to the head, "and then the opposite, death."

"Anybody know any alien code breakers?" C.C. said, looking to Mathieu.

"I could take a look."

"Later," Emily said. "I feel like everybody's mom. How many times do I have to say that this is just observation? There will be plenty of time to play with the toys, C.C."

He nodded. As the group turned to leave, they heard a giant crunching sound behind them.

C.C. had smashed the old box in.

"Oops."

"C.C.!" Emily was getting frustrated with his penchant for not following orders.

He pushed aside the broken shards of rock and wood. Inside lay a manuscript, 25 centimeters long and 33 centimeters wide. Each page was a two-centimeter-thick stone slab. C.C. lifted the heavy tome and slowly handed it to Cole. "I think this is for you. Can you read it?"

Cole leaned back to absorb the weight of the book. He traced the hieroglyphs on the cover. "*Mrititrickiliki Nafem Nafem Mrititrickiliki.* Literally, this means The Book of the Giver of Life to the World, but said backwards. The Doomsday Book."

"That sounds ominous," Mathieu said.

"Maybe, or I could be saying it wrong. I'm kind of interpreting on the fly here."

With all lights on him, he opened the dusty cover and read silently. His eyebrows furrowed. "This doesn't make any sense."

"What do you mean?"

"It's just gibberish words. The first page says 'Tok, Tok, Tok.' The second page says 'Doom, Doom, Doom.' I'm sorry, but I'm going to need more time with this."

"Time you have, but back at the Hab. We really need to get going." Emily plodded ahead.

From there, they passed by several more rooms full of scrolls, books, and ancient scientific tools. Even Emily had to stop and drool over the ancient tools and wonder what they were used for and why they were made. From there, they walked up a stone staircase to a large, open chamber.

The whole room was built around a large sphere in the middle of the room. Large oval plates stretched outward from the sphere in the center of the room. The walls were built similarly but with large stone plates dappled with small holes.

"JEVS, I hope you're getting this for Mission Data Collection," Emily said. "We are going to make a lot of astronomers happy."

The planetarium depicted the stars and moons and planets of the solar system of 51 Golgotha.

C.C. went to a plate on the wall surrounded by hieroglyphs.

"Wait, maybe we should have Cole read it first," Anna said.

C.C. pushed down on the small plate. The sound of something popping in the walls emanated through the room.

"Too late."

"You've really got to stop being so cowboy with everything," Mathieu said. Emily scowled. Cole still had his nose in the book. He only looked up when the plates in the room started to move.

"It's like a giant astronomical clock," Anna said.

"Puts Stonehenge into a whole new perspective, doesn't it?" C.C. said.

From the planetarium, they climbed more staircases that led them to the top of the wind tunnels. Before the wind tunnels, Anna stopped and turned to her right.

"What is it? Another lock box?" C.C. asked.

Anna pushed against an out-of-place stone. The wall cracked and split open. Beyond was a small room.

"This wasn't on any of the recon," Emily said. "Be careful. Everybody check your breathing equipment. I want to verify that nobody has faulty breathing apparatus before we enter a room that's been sealed for four thousand years."

After they checked their equipment and everything was working fine, Emily logged the entry for NASA, and they entered the room.

The room was thickly humid. Four bodies lay next to each other, hand-in-hand. Two of the dead were clearly children. Stone pots sat at the far side of the room. Anna opened them.

"Some of these still have food in them, or at least what I think was food," she said. She glanced around, saw a stick, and dipped it into one of the jars. A tarry substance dripped from the stick.

"What happened to them?" Mathieu said.

"And who where they hiding from, and why?" C.C. added.

"Look at the walls," Emily said.

Notches had been scratched into the far wall. She quickly counted them up. "93 notches. Were they here for 93 days?"

They took several holographic photos of the strange new find and continued to the wind tunnel.

From here, they could look out on the city. Of course, they had seen many satellite photos of Resurrection City, but never from this angle. The devastation was obvious. All the bodies, all the broken buildings, even some of the strange aqueducts that were toppled. Part of the wall had been razed during the destruction of the city.

While everyone else stared at the destruction, Cole looked back on the Calvary Mountains. On the opposite side of those peaks was the Habitation Module, but more importantly, the Ascent Vehicle. Things had changed drastically for him while journeying to Jedik-ikik. As much as he enjoyed this adventure, he really wanted to get home. There was no speeding up time, though. Home was seven years away.

Was something moving on the mountain?

Cole squinted, trying to get a better look. Maybe it was a trick of the mind, or maybe it was just weariness and gravity catching up to him, but he swore he saw something.

He was about to open his mouth when Anna said, "Mira. Down there. The Squatter."

The ground was swirling, like some invisible dust devil was grwoing out from the surface under the Squatter's statue. As the astronauts watched, little waves rippled through the dust. The waves radiated toward the walls in every direction.

Emily barked, "Everyone, we're heading out NOW!"

They rushed back downstairs, but from the floor level, they could no longer observe the ripples.

"Were they just viewable from up high?" Cole wondered.

"I don't know." Emily crossed to the epicenter. She stood over the dust and waited, but nothing happened. She reached down and pressed her fingers against the stone ripples.

"Whatever it was, it's over now," Anna said. Emily wasn't so sure.

"Where are we going next?" Mathieu asked. As he spoke, he yawned, so the words came out as one big yawn.

Emily checked on the rest of the crew. Her husband leaned against the wall of the pyramid, his head in the Doomsday Book. He was like a bulldog with a chew toy when it came to things like this. He wasn't going to let go. Anna was just as focused, but trying to figure out the riddle of the rippling dust. Her face belied her weariness. C.C. was stretching.

"We are all running on adrenaline," Emily said. "And I don't like what we just experienced, even if it's just signs of gravity-induced fatigue. So I'm adjusting the schedule. Rather than eat lunch and nap here, we're going straight to the Hab. We can eat on the way back."

C.C. rolled his eyes. Nobody else looked directly at her. Cole raised his hand.

"Um, hon, the Sunken Robot's on the way."

"C'mon," C.C. said, "we can't pass that up today." The others nodded agreement.

Emily considered it for a moment. "Okay, but a short visit. Five minutes, tops."

Nobody argued with her.

"Sweet," C.C. said.

Everyone and their DSMUs except Cole started crossing the plaza to the next nearest pyramid.

"Cole," Emily said.

"Right. Sorry." Except for raising his hand, Cole had been deep in his book the entire time.

"You okay? You look a little weird."

"I was just reading something disconcerting. This book is full of curses and warnings, straight out of a horror novel. 'Anyone who enters the City of Rebirth Without Sincerity and Peace Will Find Misery and Eternal Suffering.'"

"Ominous," C.C. said. He and the rest of the crew had stopped when Cole began reading from the Doomsday Book. "That sounds just like the warnings on the walls."

"That's here, too," Cole said. "'If you need, you will be provided. If you take, then home will be as unknown to you as the mind of the Rentok.'"

"What is a Rentok?"

"I don't know. There is more, though. Descriptions of invasion from the stars. And look." Cole held up the book. A large glyph showed a man with two arms and two legs wearing a space suit and helmet, not unlike theirs.

"Wait. Is that book predicting us?" Mathieu asked. "That's impossible. It's gotta be luck or something."

"Convergent evolution," Anna said. "It makes sense that a similar space-faring species would look like us and, thus, wear clothing like us."

"Still. That's pretty creepy," Mathieu said.

They crossed many dead bodies of the Jedik-ikik on their way to the next site. The DSMUs, in particular, struggled with walking here. The bodies were well preserved. The astronauts didn't want to damage any of them.

Cole looked up from his heavy book long enough to study the many other large buildings in Ximortikrim. They were all tall, with many second-, third-, and even fifth-floor patios. Briefly, he thought of the French Quarter in New Orleans, with all its ironwork balconies. The balconies here were stone and dust, but just as powerful a visual.

A Jedik-ikik watched him from one of the balconies. Cole jumped.

Emily, who'd been walking next to him, followed his gaze. "That's just an old dead one."

"I saw something move."

"I'll zoom in and scan it." She adjusted her scopes and stared at the balcony for a few moments. "My scopes aren't picking up anything. You sure?"

"I swear I saw something move."

Anna said, "There's no life here, and the only life on this planet is the jungle forests. We have the scans and years of satellite photography to prove it."

Emily touched Cole's arm. "Want us to skip this and return to the Hab now? Just say the word."

Cole continued to search the balconies and the columns for movement while he worked through his wife's words. "Nah. Let's keep going."

A few minutes later, they arrived at the second pyramid. Like the first pyramid, it, too was conical and tall, with wind tunnels to cool the inside. But unlike the first pyramid, this one stood at the end of several massive stone buildings. Drone study revealed this pyramid's function as the entrance to the military building of the Jedik-ikik.

"Iktit," Cole said. "Home of Ximortikrim's soldiers."

But the reason they wanted to stop here before heading back to the Hab had nothing to do with Iktit, but rather what lay outside its pyramid.

Fallen against a wall was a robot, sunk in the dust. He was a purely mechanical device full of an intricate latticework of copper and brass gears covered in stone housing. Earth's robots started the automaton once. The next five minutes of discussion before the automaton lost its power was the basis for all concept on what the language of the Jedik-ikik sounded like. Not wanting to risk damage with the robots handling the automaton, NASA elected to wait until humans could restart the machine.

Mathieu pulled out a kit designed to prepare the robot for removal from the city. He only wanted some of the brushes to clean off the dust and shine the brass and copper.

"Do you think it'll turn back on?" Anna asked.

"There's only one way to find out, but no way are we risking it by crossing our fingers and hitting the reboot button." (The reboot button, in this case, was a winding lever on the robot's chest.)

"I just want to clean him off a bit for photo work," he added. But as he brushed off the gears, he found a tiny sliver of metal jammed into the gears. The techy in him couldn't resist prying the sliver loose.

As soon as the sliver popped out, the gears began turning and whirring, kicking up a dust cloud around the robot. A fast-tempo clicking, like a metronome on high speed, was clacking back and forth in the robot's chest. The robot's head rolled up at the astronauts. Its mandibles clicked mechanically.

Cole didn't realize at first that the clicks were the robot speaking to them in the language of the Jedik-ikik.

"Wait." He addressed the robot with sudden realization. "Slow down. I can't understand you."

The robot buzzed faster.

"Um, hang on. Treek. Tiknicriki...tlikit."

The robot's head rolled to face Cole. Its mandibles slowed, almost painfully.

"Triknik. Iktit. Tiknik. Itkik. Rentok. Tok. Tok."

Cole thought a second, then said, "Quirt dridt?"

The automaton leaned forward in the dust and looked around. "Kiktikn'kikikikitl. Klint dree?"

"Nee drikliktik. Trizlipt itl tikniklitpit."

"Nee? Driktik."

Cole nodded. There were tears in his eyes.

"What's going on?" Emily asked, a little stunned. "I only picked up a few words."

Cole blinked away the tears. "He wanted to know where his family was. I told him that the Jedik-ikik died thousands of years ago. He said he is alone and cold. Nee drik. Slik klint-itl. We will be your family now."

The robot stared at Cole for a moment, then said, "Triknik iktit. Tiknik itkik. Kilil te Rentok. Rentok! Tok. Tok. Rentok!"

"What is Rentok?" C.C. asked Cole.

"I'm still not sure. He's saying something about something dark coming from the stars. Is that Rentok? Nik kil te Rentok?"

The robot looked at all the astronauts. Then it pointed back toward the mountains and said, "Rentok. Tok. Tok." The words slurred out of the robot's mouth. Its gears were winding down. The clicking in its chest had slowed.

"I wish he'd stop saying that," Anna said.

Then they heard it. An audible click from far away. But not quite a clicking sound. It sounded like metal drums beating from far away in the distance.

Tok.

Tok.

Tok.

"What was that?" C.C. said.

"Ren-tok," the robot said. It had not lowered its arm.

Tok.

Tok.

Tok.

The sound came louder.

"That's coming from the hills," Anna said.

"We need to get out of here," Emily said. "Everybody, get in your DSMUs."

"Ren...t...ok," the robot said with a final clicking in its chest.

Then the Golgothaquake hit.

CHAPTER THREE: A SEISMIC SHIFT

1

The astronauts stumbled and fell to the ground. The combination of gravity sickness and seismic activity easily toppled them, despite the astronauts' athleticism and fitness. And like any well-trained, mission-oriented team, as soon as the Golgothaquake stopped, the astronauts rose up and began working out the problems. Emily crunched satellite data while C.C. checked the seismometer in the Hab. Anna and Mathieu went to the DSMUs to verify their status.

Cole took the Doomsday Book and found a place to sit and examine the city for signs of damage. The pillars of one building crumbled, dropping the second story. Jedik-ikik statues were either leaning or fallen, but the ones around the first pyramid remained unchanged as if tethered to their spots by invisible chains. Cole mourned the loss of history. For all intents and purposes, he was the crew's historian. His task was to evaluate the findings as well as act as the crew's translator. He would guide them on which relics to return to the Anchor for portage back to Earth.

Ahead of him lay the broken remains of the largest statue in Ximortikrim. Mostly separated blocks now, the statue had once stood as tall as the highest pyramid and straddled a now crushed aqueduct. There were several theories as to what destroyed the statue, but they were nothing better than speculation. Cole's hope was to discover some clue that would tell him about the statue. For now, though, he wanted a place to sit and sift through the stone book while the others figured out what was happening. The book was so heavy. He was getting tired of holding it up.

He brushed dust off the block as he placed it on his lap. Across from him was another stone. A Jedik-ikik soldier lay fallen across the stone. He propped his feet up on another giant stone and placed the Doomsday Book carefully on his lap. When the earthquake hit, he had rolled on his

39

side to protect the book. But it was heavy, and his arms were relieved to give up the book.

The soldier stared at him from behind the two egg-like eyes on top of his head. It was more than a little unnerving. Cole thought about moving, but he didn't want to carry the book any farther, so he did his best not to look at the soldier.

On the stone below the soldier, an inscription caught his eye. Cole turned on his camera and clicked a photo of the inscription. The writing disturbed him. He did not like what it said, especially with the soldier lying there staring at him.

He got up and walked back to the group. He stopped halfway there. His eyes were to the ground to make sure that he didn't trip on a rock or slip in the dust. Something was weird about the ground, though. He couldn't figure out what was bothering him about it.

"You okay? You look like you saw a ghost." Emily walked over and placed her hand against her husband's helmet. It was the best she could do.

"This whole place is full of ghosts," Cole said.

"I think it is just the planetary acclimation getting to you. Anna and Mathieu are double-checking the DSMUs. Once we've verified they've had no damage, we're going back to the Hab."

"Good. How is 51 Golgotha?"

"The satellite didn't pick up anything abnormal, but it would've had to have been a pretty big seismic shift for the satellite to pick it up."

"Hey, guys," Mathieu called out. "We're good to go."

Cole took one more look at the ground and the dust, then he placed the Doomsday Book in the storage container and climbed into DSMU 5.

The DSMUs quickly left Ximortikrim and crossed through the jungles to the Calvary Mountains. On the path, several aftershocks registered, one big enough that the DSMUs stopped and waited it out.

"This makes no sense," C.C. said over the com. "In all our time monitoring this area, we never picked up any seismic activity. The Hab's seismometer was brought solely for geological studies to verify soundwave experiments."

"Talk to me," Emily said. "What is the seismometer saying?"

Cole could hear the business clip in her voice. Emily had shifted into problem-solver mode. She was collecting data to put together the Plan.

"The quake was a 5.8 on the Richter scale. That sounds high for what little damage we saw, but keep in mind the lack of effect of the planet's low gravity."

"And the epicenter?"

"Working on it, but I think... No." He reviewed his data. "They came from the Calvaries."

Emily looked up at the mountains. They were almost on top of them. "Okay, new plan. We're going around the mountains."

"But that will take hours," Mathieu said. "The DSMUs can take it."

"It's too risky," Emily said. "I'm calling it. JEVS, we're rerouting around the Calvary Mountain Range." She reprogrammed their route.

"Yes, sir," JEVS said.

"That's a two-hour detour," Mathieu said. "I'm not complaining. But if the goal is to return to the Hab as quickly as possible, this seems counterintuitive."

"It's worth it," C.C. said. "We don't know the power of the earthquake or its effect on the mountains. We could get halfway in and discover that the route's destroyed."

"But we have the most technologically advanced mech systems ever," Mathieu said.

"We wouldn't be the first humans to die because they thought they were stronger than what was below them. Remember the Titanic?"

"I just want to get back to the Hab already."

"We all do," Emily said.

The crew turned east. Before following the reroute with the others, Cole studied the mountain with the strange peaks. Maybe it was a trick of his mind, but he thought perhaps the peaks had shifted away from him, like they'd rolled backwards. His DSMU kneeled down and touched the ground. The rocks seemed to have folded in on themselves here. Had the ground sunk? If so, these mountains were more dangerous than Emily had predicted.

He ran after his crewmates.

Ten mountains separated the Hab from Ximortikrim. Each was a dramatic rise covered in dense alien jungle. Several posed high cliff faces that were instantly deemed insurmountable in the DSMUs.

As they made their way through dense jungle, the DSMUs switched out hands for machetes and saws that they used to cut through the vines and trees.

"These things are everywhere," Mathieu said as he pushed a tree over.

"I don't like this," Anna said. "No me cae bien."

"We knew we'd likely end up having to cross through thicket," Emily said. "That's why the DSMUs came like this."

"I know, and I understand," Anna said as she sawed through a particularly gnarly patch of vines. "I just don't like it."

The ground rumbled under their feet again.

"Everybody get low!" Emily commanded as the quake rippled through the forest. This one was much bigger and longer than the previous one. Rocks fell and trees toppled under. The rocks rose up under Cole and knocked his DSMU over.

"What the hell is happening?" Mathieu cried out.

The quake kept rolling. All the DSMUs were laid out. Rocks rolled past. Emily held her arm up to shield her from the boulders.

"Get behind me!" she shouted over the din.

While the other DSMUs scrambled to get behind her, she grabbed several boulders and positioned them as a makeshift shield against the mountain.

Cole tried reaching her, crawling across open ground while trees and dirt flew around him. He'd never experienced anything like this. He wasn't sure anyone had.

As suddenly as it began, the quake stopped.

2

When the dust settled, Emily saw her husband's badly damaged DSMU in the rubble.

"Cole!"

A dusty, black robotic hand pushed aside some boulders.

"I'm okay."

DSMU 5 stood up, then limped back to the others. One of the sensors in DSMU 5 was broken. The right hand kept switching out the robotic hand and the machete. Cole quickly overrode the sensor. Now the hand was useless.

Behind Cole, Emily saw the unbelievable. A line of light shone between the mountain and the ground beneath it. Giant roots as thick as pipelines stretched between the ground and the mountain.

"What do you see?" C.C. asked.

"I really don't know. This doesn't make sense," Emily said. "I think the mountain rose up."

C.C. pushed her aside and surveyed the damage.

"That's impossible."

"We need to get back to the city," Emily said.

"No, the Hab. We will be better protected there," C.C. countered.

"Those mountains are between us and the Hab."

"We can still make it around them."

"Do the math. That will take hours. We don't have that kind of time. We don't know what's going to happen. We are returning to Ximortikrim. We will regroup there and analyze the situation. JEVS, the crew is repositioning to Ximortikrim. Seismic activity has caused unusual and dangerous deviations among the mountains. I am concerned for the crew's safety, so I am moving them."

"I am analyzing the data to determine the locus and cause of the seismic activity," JEVS said.

C.C. wanted to protest, but another quake rumbled to life under their feet. The DSMUs stumbled as they retreated to Ximortikrim.

3

While they ran, Cole looked behind him. What he saw made him stop and made him want to run faster at the same time. Seeing his reaction, everyone else stopped, too.

They could not believe their eyes. Science had no answer to what they saw.

Two kilometers behind them, the mountain continued to rise, shaking dust and rocks and trees. Sections of rock broke free and stretched outward.

Like arms, Cole thought.

A sheer bluff face split open. Craggy teeth chomped at the air. Massive shoulders rolled back, exposing a thick, sharp head.

"That's not real," Anna said.

The quake stopped rumbling. The giant monster put two immense hands on the peaks of the mountains beside it and roared. It sounded like wrenching metal and fingers being dragged down a blackboard. Cole cringed.

"What the hell is that?" C.C. asked.

Emily grabbed him by the shoulder. "We've got to go."

But they couldn't leave. They were too much in awe of the gigantic mountain monster. In a cloud of dust of its own making, the creature turned to face them.

"We've definitely got to go."

This time, everybody followed her.

Behind them, the massive creature pulled its arms back, like it was stretching its shoulders. As its arms moved, white and blue chain lightning erupted from its chest. The creature made a hissing sound as it moved its arms back and forth, growing the lightning seed in its chest. Electricity highlighted the creature's crevices.

Suddenly, the DSMUs found themselves running through a forest of lightning. Bolts shrieked through the air and spiked into the ground. The astronauts did their best to dodge the electric icicles. C.C. took a bolt to the chest. It exploded in white and blue fire. When the forest of lightning stopped, so did C.C.'s DSMU. Emily ran back to him.

"I can't move," C.C. shouted.

The lights on DSMU 2 were out. The power was down in his DSMU. He tried hitting the backup power button. Nothing. His system was completely fried.

She motioned to the others. Mathieu helped her lift the frozen DSMU and carry it across the valley. The giant monster's roars followed them through the gates of Ximortikrim.

CHAPTER FOUR: RISE OF THE RENTOK

1

"Mathieu, get that DSMU working again. Anna and Cole, find us a good hiding place. JEVS, there is a giant…monster rising up. What we thought were mountains. We were wrong. I am broadcasting my live feed so that you can record it, too."

"Emily," Cole said.

"Hold on a second." Emily opened her cockpit and stood up to see the giant monster better. The creature pumped its two legs, like it was stuck in quicksand.

Anna had already begun to search the military compound. Cole had his own idea of where they should go, but all he could think about was the inscription next to the soldier. "Between the nevers, the dead lie dreaming," he said aloud.

"What was that?" Emily asked.

"Something I read. An inscription." But now he was staring at something that made his skin crawl.

"Emily," he said again. His tone was sharp and clipped.

"I'm filming the monster for Mission Data Collection and for analysis later. Have you found a safe place?"

"I have. I've found something else. First contact."

"What?" she turned around. Cole's DSMU stood frozen in place, staring back at the broken dome. This was the place she figured he meant for hiding. But about fifty meters in front of Cole stood another creature. It was a dust-covered homo-insectus, and it was definitely alive. It carried a spear in one hand as it sneered at the astronauts.

The homo-insectus shouted something angry in its bug language.

"What'd it say?" Emily asked.

"You've awakened the Rentok."

The thing turned and ran back toward the dome, beating the end of his spear in the ground as he shouted over and over, "Krit! Krit! Krit!"

"Arise! Arise! Arise!"

"It's heading to the dome. We've got to follow it," Emily said. "Mathieu!"

"I'm almost done. I had to tether the two DSMUs together. The batteries are completely fried. We will both have less power, but the DSMUs will be able to move."

"Good, cause that thing's coming this way. We've got to get out of here."

Indeed, the monster had finally freed itself of the ground and taken the first step toward Ximortikrim and the astronauts.

"Go! Go! Go!" she shouted to the other astronauts. Anna's DSMU was running from the military compound. Cole waited for Emily, then ran to the dome. Mathieu and C.C. brought up the rear.

Cole saw the Jedik-ikik dodging around a corner and entering the dome. On the one hand, Cole was glad that he was no longer seeing things that weren't there, but then again, he wished he'd never seen the four-armed man.

The dome was split asunder down the side, damage from a meteoroid hit. Three craters were still visible from satellite pictures of the city, and one meteor had hit close enough to destroy half of the dome. In the middle of the room was a large shaft built on a free-rotating ball. The shaft, which was covered in ancient hieroglyphics, reached from the floor to the cracked ceiling.

The DSMUs easily entered under its tall roof, which was held together by hexagonal beam support covered by the same black granite the aliens used for the rest of their architecture.

"Where did it go?" Cole asked as they entered the dome.

"There," Emily said, pointing to a stairwell. To her, everything about the culture read "mud dauber." Even something as simple as a stairwell was more like a tunnel stuck to the framework of the outside building. She was getting out of the DSMU to chase after the bug when they heard another clicking sound. The alien had stopped his angry shouting. Up in his room, he stuck his spear into a console and pulled the lever.

Outside of his wall, the hexagonal structure began swirling. Emily saw now that the beams weren't just simple hexagons but had little gears at the corners so that the hexagons could spin. As the hexagons moved, so did the dome.

"What's it doing?" C.C. asked. He was now out of his DSMU, too.

Before anyone could respond, a series of loud booms resonated like thunder through the room.

The monster was approaching.

From somewhere else came a groaning sound, like giant winches pushing against time and rust. Cole didn't like the sound of them. They sounded like they were about to break.

"What do we do?" he asked his wife.

She pointed to the shaft, which was slowly rotating in their direction.

"Anyone else feel like they're staring down a really big ass gun?" Mathieu asked.

The astronauts fled from the barrel just as a bright redness appeared deep inside.

Emily charged across the field of dead soldiers to the first pyramid. Ahead of them, the giant monster watched them run. It was a silhouette on the horizon, a tall mountain peak rising above all others.

Inside his DSMU, Cole was going through his words, trying to stay calm. "Mellifluous. Mellifluous. Tincture. Calm. Balanced." The words came out as short gasps while he watched the mountain of a monster begin to pull its arms back. Its eyes were glowing like electric lightbulbs on a Christmas display.

"We've got about ten seconds before that thing recharges," Emily shouted. "Move!"

We can make it, she thought to herself. It wasn't just positive vibes. Her plan was to get to the far side of the pyramid, regroup, and find a path out of there that would not get the monster's attention. The corner was not that far away. They could make it.

Mathieu dragged C.C. behind them. He was falling far behind the others.

"Emily!"

She turned and saw her two crewmen falling back. She ran back to get them. She lifted C.C.'s DSMU in her arms and began running. As she did, the tether between the two DSMUs popped. Mathieu surged forward with extra energy.

She could feel the electricity biting the air. She dared not look back.

DOOOM!

A loud noise boomed through Ximortikrim. The blast was so powerful, the mechs' knee joints buckled. The DSMU's sprawled out, knocked down.

Before they could get up, a cacophony of sound and rumbling waves pushed over the crew.

Behind them, the monster lay on the ground, his shoulder smoking and badly damaged. The electric charge burst around him. Lightning gouged through the earth and sky.

"What the hell just happened?"

Cole pointed to the dome and its smoking barrel. "The dome. It was their weapon against the monsters."

"Well, now we have cover. Let's get out of here."

"There is no other way out of here," Mathieu said. "We have to go through the main gate."

"No, there is another gate. Right, Cole?"

"No, there isn't. Ximortikrim has only the one serviceable entrance, and all outer walls are 30 meters tall."

"Right, but the wall is not entirely up, remember? Come on."

They ran after her, charging to the western outer wall.

"JEVS, do you read me?" Emily said into her com.

"Go ahead, Commander Musgrove."

"Move the Anchor into orbit over Ximortikrim and the Hab. Be ready in case we need to evacuate."

"Yes, sir."

Cole called out to his wife. "Baby, the parts of the wall that were destroyed were near the entrance."

Anna chimed in. "Does anybody else think this giant thing is the reason for all the damage to the city?"

"Way ahead of you there," C.C. said. "While I've been down, I've been re-examining the topo maps."

"Will you all shut up?" Cole shouted. "Emily, the wall! What are you talking about?"

"It's what you were talking about, love. I remember about a month ago you were going over the maps. You were wondering what happened to the front gate that caused the damage. The going theory, if you remember, was war."

Cole's eyes lit up. "Of course!"

"Ja, I don't understand," Mathieu said.

"One of the reasons for the war theory was a false wall to the west. Almost invisible to the naked eye, but the gate was open. Several Jedi-ikik were found dead there, leading to the conclusion that this was a passage for escaping the city should it fall."

"I think this counts as falling," Anna said. "Let's get out of here."

2

The gate was open a crack. Dead (*Or dreaming*, Cole thought) homo-insectus lay scattered on both sides of the wall. One of them seemed strange to Cole. The home-insectus had some markings on its face that he did not comprehend. He had no time to collect data. They had to escape the city before the giant monster entered it. Cole looked behind. They were shielded out of sight because of a rise of buildings. This, of course, was more evidence to support the hidden passage theory. Clearly, the Jedik-ikik did not want this passage seen from the front entrance.

"We need to head north," C.C. said as they exited the city.

Emily was perplexed. "North? There's nothing north of here."

"A city. It is far to the north, but we can go there."

"Like, a thousand kilometers to the north," Cole said.

Emily said, "No, we need to return to the Hab. There, we have supplies, tools, food, and most importantly, the Ascent Vehicle. We don't know what is out there."

Cole added, "What is not out there is a monster the size of the Statue of Liberty. We can lose it in the jungles, and we can use the ascent capability in the DSMUs to return to orbit."

"I like that idea," Mathieu said.

"So do I," Anna added. "But biologically speaking, the Hab's our best chance of survival. We're all beat up from yesterday's descent, and now all this. We're running on adrenaline and fumes, and once those give in, we won't be capable of dealing with whatever we find in the unknown. We can't count on ourselves right now, biologically speaking."

"But," C.C. started to say, but Emily cut him off.

"This isn't a democracy. This isn't Palo Duro, and we aren't kids, C.C. I'm the commander. We all have a mission, and we are still on that mission, which means I'm still in charge. JEVS, relay this to Mission Data Collection: the crew has fled the city after the appearance of a giant stone monster. We will rendezvous with the Hab for observation and ascent, if need be."

The astronauts cut vines and foliage to camouflage their DSMUs. They then crouched low to the ground and made their way slowly along the wall. Above them, the giant monster towered. It was searching for them near the city wall.

A giant chunk of the monster's shoulder was missing. A small patch, the center of the impact, was more badly damaged than the others. Here, they saw a chink in the monster's armor. A small patch of green skin shined through. The monster did not move its broken arm as it searched for the astronauts.

The DSMUs moved slowly through the trees, careful not to shake them lest they attract the monster's eye.

Emily took them back to the Calvary Mountains.

"We aren't seriously going there, are we?" C.C. asked. "That thing was a mountain, remember?"

"We don't have a choice. It's the quickest way back to the Hab."

"There is always a choice," C.C. shot back.

"You have no power, C.C., so you can't see what the rest of us see. The DSMUs are low on power. They weren't designed for extended running. And we are all beat up physically and mentally. That's obvious from the health monitors. We are way over our stress limits. It is almost 1600 hours. We have missed lunch, and now first dinner. The suits are recommending immediate rest and food."

DOOOM!!!

A second blast resounded across the valley. The astronauts had started to climb the mountain with the strange peaks when the Jedik-ikik's weapon surged a second time. This time, they had a good view of the blast. Plumes of smoke shot out of one end, and a small rocket out of the other. This time, the giant monster stepped away from the cannon fire. The rocket scorched over the valley and crashed into one of the mountains. A giant face of the mountain exploded. The mountainside began to cave in on itself, causing an enormous rock slide. The DSMUs held on to trees for balance while the mountain recoiled from the hit and the dust cleared.

A giant patch of skin lay beneath the rocks.

"We need to get off this mountain," Anna said.

"Right."

But the monster had already seen them. As it twisted to dodge the attack, its electric eyes caught the white of the DSMUs. The creature rolled its shoulders back and pulled back its arms.

"Run!" Emily said.

Cole was going out of his mind. He wished he'd never left the comfort of his professorship in Austin. He would be home with Emily and his nephew, and he certainly wouldn't be running through an alien jungle, scaling a mountain that may or may not be a giant monster, while being shot at by lightning bolts by another impossibly gigantic rock monster.

Lightning burst from the center of the creature's chest. Electric chains sidewinded through the sky, crashing into the mountain. Like the others, he could feel his hairs standing on end just before the lightning storm hit them. He didn't have time to wonder if this was out of fear or if it was because of the increased amount of electricity in the air.

A blue cord flashed in front of him. Cole stopped in his tracks to avoid the burn. Then he jumped over a bright white heat just as it struck the ground where he'd been standing. It was like trying to escape the effects of a massive Tesla coil. He hoped he'd live.

3

Somehow, unbelievably, they all survived the lightning storm. They'd reached the mountain's serrated peaks. They could see the Ascent Vehicle on the other side.

"OGRA," Emily said into her com, "I want all drones to follow the monster and record its movement. Keep a distance of at least fifty meters from the monster. Have the video ready to play when we get back to the Hab."

"Yes, Commander Musgrove." The four drones pushed wide to video the monster.

Tok.

Tok.

Tok.

"Oh, no," Cole said.

The mountain shuddered.

"Did you hear that?" C.C. asked.

"I felt it," Mathieu said.

Emily jumped down off the peak 6 meters to the next lower steps. "Keep moving!"

Like a robotic mountain goat, she hopped, stepped, and maneuvered down the mountainside. She was thankful for the robustness of her mech's gyroscopes. They were the only thing keeping her from stumbling into a roll and falling off the shifting mountain. Rocks tumbled around her as more aftershocks threw the astronauts to the ground.

"I don't think the DSMUs were designed for this," Cole said.

"We're in ops reserve mode now, Cole," Emily said. "Design is off the table."

Cole took her DSMU's hand in his, and they both jumped off a cliff face. The problem was not that they hit the ground but that the ground hit them. The rock rose up to hit them. The two DSMUs fell back onto the ledge with C.C., Anna, and Mathieu.

The mountain monster was rising up, and they were no more than little birds on its back.

The creature roared. Its voice was dark and loud and sounded like a hundred heavy metal concerts going on at the same time. The creature was so immense they could not see its head. But they could feel the pressure change as the mountain rose up in the sky. Within seconds, they were a few hundred meters higher in the air than they were before. Emily's ear popped.

"Well, there goes the climbing option," Cole said.

"There's more than one way to get off this mountain," Emily said. She reached down and pressed a button on her mech's lower legs. The three panels shot off, exposing robust rocket launchers.

"You can't be serious," Mathieu said. "Even if we'd done the math and tracked the flight, those are one-time use *solid* rocket boosters. Once ignited, there's no stopping them. They'll launch us out of the atmosphere, and then what?"

To respond, Emily ripped off the connecting plate on her lower rocket boosters and removed the upper boosters. "That should be enough to get us off the mountain."

"Should be?" Anna asked, credulous. "Now you're sounding like your husband."

Emily looked at Cole. "I'll take that as a compliment."

"How the hell do we steer?" Mathieu shouted over the rumbling mountain. The mountain twisted, nearly knocking the astronauts over the ledge.

"The same way I steered during EDL. Use the Abort Landing screen to give manual control of the DSMU to you."

"And what? Fly like Superman?"

To respond, she handed C.C.'s mech to Anna. Emily grabbed her husband's DSMU by the waist.

Inside his DSMU, Cole was frantically grabbing his shoulder harness and locking himself down.

"Shit, baby, not again!"

Emily leaned down. Sparks shot from her DSMU's hands, lighting the solid rocket boosters. In a spray of sparks and vapor and flame, she and Cole launched off the mountain.

Emily was smiling.

4

The first three seconds were fine because the rockets shot straight up. After that, everything went to hell in a handbasket. Unlike ascent/descent, where the direction of travel is mostly up or down, Emily was trying to steer herself southward, which meant flying horizontally. The SRBs didn't like that, and the laws of aerodynamics were not in her favor. Her mech was not built with flight in mind, so control was a joke. They were going wherever the laws of physics took them. She quickly learned to stiffen the arms and legs of the mobility unit and use slight changes in the SRBs to create lift along a horizontal plane. This stabilized her craft after six loops in the air that had culminated in a dive-bomb straight to the ground that was as graceful as a first-time RC plane enthusiast.

That they did not die was due at least in part to how high they were when they started their escape. If they had tried this from sea level, she was pretty sure they would have collided into the ground.

But she was off the mountain.

Suddenly, Emily pulled out, and they were flying.

"I think I puked in my helmet," Cole said.

"Don't get comfortable. I still need to figure out how to land this thing before we overshoot the landing site by a continent or two. Don't worry, though. I've got an idea."

"I hope it's not like New Orleans."

"No, no. New Orleans was totally different. Well, mostly."

"We crashed!"

"But I've learned so much since then. Trust me, Cole."

Cole checked his straps.

The DSMU was built with over three dozen individual "eyeholes" around the suit's "head." This was the ARGES System. ARGES was short for Augmented Reality Global Exploration System, and it allowed the DSMU pilot to see 360 degrees at all times. Because of the ARGES, Emily could see that the rest of her crew had escaped the mountain.

The mountain itself was something out of a monster movie. The peaks were the spine of the long creature, which was so massive that it dwarfed the lightning monster. It had long stalagmite and stalactite teeth, giant claws, and a long tail.

The two monsters ignored the crew. They were focused on the city, which was fine by Emily. As they marched to Ximortikrim, Emily hoped to survive long enough to see the footage. Why were they attacking the city, and why were the inhabitants of the city rising up from the grave? There were mysteries to solve. She hoped to live to find the answers.

She switched out her hand with her machete. She swung the machete at her left leg. The swing made her DSMU spin, but once she connected with the SRB, the booster went flying off. She swung at the other SRB, and it went flying off, too.

"Great. Now we're falling," Cole said.

As high up as they were (Cole's altimeter read 2000 meters), Cole knew that this was not a safe height for parachuting, much less doing whatever the hell they were doing. Emily struggled to push her hands and legs forward, fighting against the drag of air coming up against the DSMU. With all her weariness weighing on her, she struggled to move her appendages. She grunted and growled as she forced her appendages forward.

Cole guessed they had twenty seconds before they would be set on a collision course with the ground, and no matter what his wife did, there would be no escape. No last second pull-out.

"Come on!" Emily shouted as she forced the arms slowly outward.

"Push harder," Cole said. He reached out for her arms, but being slung over her back, he didn't have many options to help. He could try to push her legs down and hit his emergency landing oxygen release tanks.

Ten seconds.

He pushed hard, but the drag was too much. He just wasn't in the right position for saving them. Emily had the angle of attack that could work. Outside, sonic booms ricocheted. They were breaking the sound barrier.

"You've got to do this, Emily. I don't want to feel the back of my skull coming through the front of my skull."

She grunted something. Slowly, her arms and legs moved in the right direction.

Five seconds.

Her right arm snapped back, like she'd touched a hot wire.

Three seconds.

"Screw it. Punch it!" Emily said. She hit the emergency landing button and hoped that her arms and legs didn't rip the suit apart.

BSHHHHH!!!

The sound was like fire ripping from a flamethrower. It was thick and full of energy.

They didn't die, and her arms and legs weren't ripped apart. She could feel the difference in drag, the pause of lift under her DSMU's chest. She hit the emergency landing button again. Oxygen ejected from the arms and legs of her DSMU.

They didn't come to a gentle landing, but the DSMUs weren't obliterated, either. They rolled (per their descent programming) to a safe location and stood up, covered in dust and carbon burns.

Cole fell to his knees.

Emily checked her DSMU's readings. "Cole, we made fifteen hundred kilometers per hour. That's the record for fastest freefall. Certainly the record for fastest freefall on 51 Golgotha."

Cole was retching again. "That was like a roller coast without a track."

Around them, Anna and Mathieu landed easily, feet first.

"How'd you do that?" Emily asked.

"Emergency shutoff screen. We tried relaying it to you, but I don't think you heard," Mathieu said.

They watched as the two giant monsters moved toward Ximortikrim.

"All this effort to get here to study a new alien culture, and they're going to pulverize it," Cole said.

Emily put her hand on his shoulder, and he took her hand in his. The other three climbed out of their DSMUs while OGRA's robots brought the DSMUs to the recharge stations.

"I want these samples analyzed tonight," C.C. told Anna. "This expedition is going down the tubes, and I don't want to come home empty-handed. We still have a company to support."

The JEVS aboard the Anchor pinged Emily as she walked into the Hab. Every step felt like moving through a strong snowstorm. Her feet hurt. She could barely pull them up the stairs without stumbling on the steps.

Inside, Emily popped off her helmet and dumped it on the floor. The smell of the Hab (peppermint, as determined by the Human Performance people back in Houston) was fresh in her nose. It was a much better smell than the one coming from her suit. She'd been running and flying in the AXES for over ten hours now.

Her crew looked as deflated as Emily felt. They had gone way over budget on personal energy reserves, and that would have been on a day when they were fully rested. None of them had slept well the previous night, and they were all up early in the morning. They needed sleep.

"Everyone, we need to rest."

"But Ximortikrim," Cole said.

"I have analysis to complete," Anna added.

Emily looked into their tired, baggy eyes and said, "OGRA can monitor the monsters and finish your analysis. She'll alert us if they head this way. But right now, we all need to sleep."

She dimmed the lights. Cole was watching the devastation on the monitors. The creatures were moving toward Ximortikrim. Every step was a small bump in the Hab. Emily turned off the monitor screen. Cole followed her to her room. They pulled off their AXES suits and fell into bed together, instantly asleep.

5

The Hab's gentle shaking woke Emily. She quickly turned on a screen to check on the monsters. The bedroom's side screen showed not two, but now three giant monsters standing among the mountains, giant pits all that were left from where they had lain. The monsters were staring at a fourth mountain, but nothing was happening.

Cole was still sound asleep. She moved his arm off her shoulder and slipped out from underneath him. She checked the time. 0500 hours. Had she really slept that long? She stretched from her back to her ankles. It was one of those really good morning stretches. The kind that starts slow and ends up moving through the entire body. She twisted her neck, popping it, and brushed back her short, punky hair.

She grabbed a towel and entered her shower. The water, which was superheated at the ISRU Station, was already hot when she turned on the faucet.

While she showered, she pulled up the shower screen so she could keep an eye on them. The giant monsters would shift their weight while they stood over the fourth mountain. With each step, the Hab shook a little. *We will need a name for the creatures*, Emily thought. If C.C. was going to have an extinct animal named for him, maybe she could get one of these monsters named for her. *The Musgrovesaur, or Emily-zilla.* Then again, maybe they should leave the name-picking to the biologist.

She checked with JEVS, who had pinged her as she arrived in the Hab last night. JEVS did not respond, which was a little odd, but she guessed he was on the far side of the planet. In a few minutes, he would be back in radio contact and ready to talk about last night's ping. She assumed it was just to let her know that the Anchor had moved into the requested orbit.

She went back to the drones and surveyed Ximortikrim. She nearly slipped in the shower, she was so shocked.

"Cole," she called out.

He mumbled and threw a pillow at her.

On the screen, Ximortikrim was flurrying with activity, like an anthill that had been stepped on or a beehive that had been whacked like a piñata. Thousands of the Jedik-ikik were now alive and running around the city. The dome and the military compound were the two busiest buildings, but every building, including the First Pyramid, was buzzing. The Jedik-ikik were preparing for war. But it was more than that. Some of the Jedik-ikik were being laid out against walls and killed, spears to the head. She wasn't sure what was going on, but she knew everyone needed to see this.

"OGRA, please wake everyone," Emily said. "The city is...is alive. We need to make preparations. I think a war is about to break out."

OGRA said, "The rest of the crew is already awake, except for Cole."

"What?"

"Doctors Anna Altieri, Mathieu De Pleises, and Chris 'C.C.' Crenshaw are already awake."

"Location?"

"Dr. Anna Altieri is in the main room, and Doctors Mathieu De Pleises and Chris 'C.C.' Crenshaw are returning from the Geological Survey Rover to the Hab."

Emily shut off the shower, toweled herself off, and put on her mission suit. "Cole, wake up," she said, pushing down on the bed.

"It's Story time," he said, half in a dream.

"Cole," Emily said again, this time more sternly. Cole's eyes fluttered open. Seeing his wife's demeanor, he bolted up.

"What's wrong?"

"I don't know. Get up. The rest of the crew is already awake."

"The monsters?"

"They're no current danger to us."

"Wait. Then what's the problem?" He rolled his fists around his eyes and yawned.

"I don't know. But I can feel it. Can't you?"

He blinked his eyes.

"Get dressed."

Emily went into the main room. C.C. and Mathieu had just entered the Hab. They were still in their AXES suits, looking at something Anna was showing them.

"Good morning," Emily said, not sure where to start.

C.C. glanced up at her, then went back to counseling Anna. "That is good work, Anna. I want you to send that back to the Anchor."

"The Anchor is on the far side of the planet. You can't reach it," Emily said.

Anna glanced at Emily before asking C.C., "Do you think we can begin today?"

"We'll have to. Mathieu, you have the Ascent Vehicle prepped?"

Mathieu nodded.

"Prepped?" Emily asked, shocked. "Who told you to prep the Ascent Vehicle?"

C.C. exhaled. On the table, he pulled up a message and flipped it around so that she could read it. She recognized it as Charter Eighteen.

"What is this?" she asked. She knew what it was for, but wasn't sure why it was being invoked.

Finally, C.C. looked Emily in the eye.

"What's up?" Cole asked as he walked sleepily out of their room, pulling his t-shirt over his head.

"C.C. is taking back command."

"But we're on the ground. You're commander on the ground, babe."

Emily pointed at her husband while glaring at C.C. His eyes were white pits in dark smudges, and his facial stubble was showing.

She said, "You're drained. You haven't slept. You're not mentally capable of making this kind of decision."

"Maybe she's right," Anna said.

C.C. said, "I only have to be mentally competent enough to follow the processes and procedures developed for this mission. We've found diamonds. A large mine of them. And we've found evidence of thulium and lutenium, too. And not only that, but Anna's analysis is showing the potential of the plants here for real groundbreaking pharmaceutical work. Like, new kinds of morphine and Alzheimer's drugs kinds of pharmaceutical work. This place is a veritable Garden of Eden of possibilities, and that's not including the possibility of resurrection that we still haven't cracked. We're hitting it out of the ballpark, Em. Under Charter Eighteen, that gives Titan Space the right to take control of the mission."

"Where is your proof? You can't just take control like this, C.C. There's protocols to follow."

"Processes, man," Cole added. "You know, the ones you're just following."

"Right." He opened fifteen more files from the tabletop and flipped them to Emily. "Start reading."

Then he hailed Mission Data Collection in Houston, saying, "JEVS, I have a message for Mission Data Collection."

"JEVS is offline and out of reach," Emily said.

"I'm here, Commander," JEVS said.

"What?" She looked at C.C. Realization seeped in. JEVS was a deliverable of Titan Space.

C.C. said, "This is Anchor Commander C.C. Crenshaw. I am in the Habitation Module with the rest of the crew. It is Day 3 on 51 Golgotha. I am reporting that I am taking command of the mission under Charter Eighteen, which grants Titan Space the authority to take control of the mission should sufficient, viable resources be discovered on 51 Golgotha a."

"You need her acceptance," Mathieu said.

C.C.'s eyes furrowed.

"I'm just saying. That's the process."

Emily said, "JEVS, I'm not ready to relieve command to Titan Space. More review of the analysis work is needed. Also, there is a substantial native species threat to the north of us."

"Wait, what threat?" Cole asked.

Emily continued. "As the NASA Commander, it is my duty to remove those threats before the crew moves forward with further analysis of the southern mountains. Once the threat is removed, I will re-evaluate the change in command."

"Yes, sir," JEVS said.

"You can't do that," C.C. said.

"I just did."

"You always do that. Change the rules so that you win."

"Don't be so petulant. And just because you don't know the rules doesn't mean I'm changing them."

"So is anybody going to elaborate on the word 'threat' and what that means?" Cole asked.

"Screw this," C.C. said. He walked back to his room.

To Anna and Mathieu, she said, "You all need rest. You've seen the city, right? You know something is going down." For her husband, she flicked up the drone camera views. He covered his mouth in awe.

To the rest of the crew, she continued, saying, "I don't want to be hasty, but if we are forced to leave, we'll need our wits about us, so you three, go get some shut eye. Yesterday was a taxing day that you all worsened by being up all night. We can discuss analyses after you've slept."

Anna nodded. She and Mathieu went back to their respective rooms and shut the doors behind them.

Cole said, "So early morning mutiny tempered by sane minds. Are you sure we will be okay?" he asked, nodding to the views of Ximortikrim.

Emily said, "We are more than several kilometers away, and I think that these two groups, the giant monsters and the newly alive Jedik-ikik, are fighting each other. They don't care about us."

"Possibly, or possibly they are working together to get rid of us."

"You don't really believe that, do you?"

"I believe that our coming here precipitated all of this."

"Me, too."

Cole clapped his hands together. "Well, after that mood-killer, I still want eggs. You?"

She shook her head no and sat down to read C.C.'s evidence. This couldn't be. And while it was not a "mutiny," it was a massive deviation from the plan, which riled her. She needed to study Titan Space's evidence. If there was substantial evidence to support their theories, then maybe there was an opening for returning command to C.C. She didn't like the notion. She felt like she'd only just gotten control of the team. But if the procedure fit, she wouldn't stand in its way.

Cole hugged her around her shoulders. "I'm sorry, Emily. Is there anything I can do?"

"Say hello to the chickens for me."

6

The Animal Station stood thirty meters from the Habitation Module. One of the OGRA robots met him at the door of the Habitation Module.

"Would you like me to get the eggs for you?" the robot asked.

"No. I need the fresh air," he said.

"The air is mostly carbon monoxide. It is not fresh."

"Thank you, OGRA."

"You're welcome. Let me know if I can be of any assistance."

Cole crossed the open area to the Animal Station. He'd been looking forward to this moment for at least three years. Sharing space with the woman of his dreams was the joy of a lifetime, but he'd been anticipating the chance to see another animal besides his four cohorts.

He took some chickenfeed and spread it on the ground. While the birds plucked at the chickenfeed, he picked up one of the little chicks and held it in his hand. As the little ball of yellow feathers searched his hand for feed, she tickled Cole. He laughed and put the chick back on the ground.

"Emily, you gotta come see this," he said over the com.

The airlock opened.

"Already here."

Twenty seconds later, Emily entered the Animal Station. She sat next to her husband, holding his hand while they admired the simplicity of life playing out before them. They stayed out in the Animal Station for hours. Caring for the animals took their minds off the problems of the rest of the world. It was weird, how chores relaxed them. OGRA kept insisting she could complete the work, but they thanked her and kept working.

Cole asked, "Why do I love this so much?"

"Things have gotten really complex really quickly here. I think it is the simplicity that you admire."

"Maybe."

"Is it something else?"

"I think I miss our planet. I think I miss our nephew."

"I know, babe."

"He's only four years old now."

She squeezed Cole's hand lovingly, then began softly rubbing his fingers. She could hear everything he wasn't saying. How guilty he felt that his sister died, how horrible he felt that he wasn't able to be there to raise his own flesh and blood. How scared he was that his grandparents would die before they finally returned.

"He'll be fourteen when we get back."

"We're going to get back, Emily. I don't care if the whole planet is covered in diamonds and giant monsters, we're getting back to him. I was happy when it was just you and me, and I liked that life, but now that I know he is out there without his mother... We need to get back to him."

She hugged and kissed her husband while the chickens clucked around them.

"There's something else," Cole added. "I've been doing some reading. I don't think the resurrection agent is everything C.C. hoped it would be."

"What do you mean?"

"The Doomsday Book makes reference to a plan in the case that the Rentok attack. The Rentok are those giant monsters we saw. They have tried attacking the Jedik-ikik several times. So the Jedik-ikik developed this bacteria that causes creatures to fall into a catatonic state. They meant to use it against the Rentok, but something went wrong, and it must have zapped the entire city as well as the Rentok."

"Wow. That's great, Cole. I know you want to be back home with Story, but I'm so glad you are here with me. I need you by my side, figuring things out like this." She kissed him.

The ground shook violently. This wasn't a giant shifting its weight.

"Did you feel that?" she asked.

"Oh, yeah. Let's try again." He pulled her back to his lips, but she put her hand over his mouth.

"No, it wasn't us."

Emily looked up to the skies, expecting to see a giant monster looking into the Animal Station. There wasn't any, but the chickens had fled back to their coups.

The ground rumbled again. "Let's get back in the Hab," she said.

7

Inside the Hab, the rest of the crew already awake. For having less than three or four hours of sleep, they seemed very alert, if not a little disheveled. As Emily and Cole walked in, Anna pulled her hair back in a band. C.C. and Mathieu were sitting around the table, watching the monitor screens blankly.

"Things are about to go really south on us," C.C. said. He sipped some coffee. "You need to see this."

He didn't sound angry or bitter, which Emily appreciated. He was respecting the chain of command even if he was not ready to concede the loss.

Cole and Emily looked down on the monsters shown on the table top.

8

The Jedik-ikik military took up their blunt-nosed spears. The undead came together in formation behind the wall. Beneath their clawed feet was the spiral that meant everything in their lives, deaths, and rebirths. Eternity was a spiral as simple and eloquent as a conch shell and as complicated as a galaxy. Now was their time to take their part in the spiral.

A shadow spread across the Jedik-ikik warriors. The shadow grew as the mountains rose up before them, first above the giant wall, and then over their beloved city. Three heads from three separate monsters climbed into the sky. First, the electric-eyed raven, K't'chimigalpa-kiritikikikee k'tang. At his side stood that other monster from the stars. But behind them rose the slumbering chaos that was mighty Renslot, the largest and most reviled of the Rentok. Renslot, Destructor of Worlds. Renslot, Curse of the Cosmos.

"Trik likniklee," the warriors' sergeants said. *Take heed and be ready.*

Every roar of the Rentok was a thunderhead. Every step, a quake that moved stone. And still, the Jedik-ikik warriors did not move. They knew what death was coming for them. Mistakes had been made. Atonement was needed, and they would make the sacrifice.

"Zree! Tleeekt!" shouted one young warrior as he threw down his blunt-nosed spear and ran from the approaching mountain gods.

"Kape mitigist!" cursed one of the sergeants. He reached over and grabbed the frightened child with one of his claws. At any other time, he might have sent the child home to his mother. But this was not that time. He slammed his spear into the child's head. A concussive blast of energy shattered the child-soldier's exoskeleton and squashed it like paper.

"Nee Drik t'likicree," the sergeant told the soldiers around him. There would be no remorse for cowards because the gods had deemed only one way out of this mess. This was grim business. The only light in it came from the dome behind them. That light surged red, and it would bring death with it.

A deafening roar as loud as a hurricane blasted over and through the soldiers. Renslot was ready to take Ximortikrim.

K'tang pulled electricity from his chest to rain down on one large group of soldiers. They ran, trying to escape, but the barrage was too much for them.

"Kree! Kriktik!" shouted their general from his post at the military tower high above the soldiers.

The soldiers ran to the monsters.

K'tang and Zree stepped over the giant wall. Zree's first step crunched a patrol of Jedik-ikik warriors. K'tang kicked over the thick wall as he entered. Rock and boulders exploded over the Jedik-ikik, crushing and killing the soldiers in its path. One of the rocks bounced until it slammed into the First Pyramid, narrowly missing the statue guardians.

"Kree! Kree!" cried the general, encouraging his troops to continue moving to the monsters.

The Jedik-ikik swarmed like fire ants over Zree's four legs. His rocky legs were as hot as embers, yet still they climbed up and up, using their clawed hands and feet to find purchase.

The giant monster pushed forward across the spiral and kicked through an array of giant columns. It took a swing at a pyramid, knocking the top half off. Jedik-ikik who had been hiding in the temple screamed as they fell to their deaths.

Zree pushed into a thick-walled hall.

Below, the sergeant released a pheromone to signal his soldiers in arms to finally attack. Fifty soldiers stabbed the monster's legs with their blunt-nosed spears, surprising it with a flurry of concussive blasts. A thunder peal of agony ripped across the valley. The soldiers kept stabbing and stabbing.

A thick cloud of ash and bloomed out of the monster's eyes. It leaned down with its long neck and spewed lava from its mouth. Jedik-ikik were incinerated instantaneously under the fiery rock. The soldiers on the Zree's other legs worked faster, knowing death was reaching out to them. The monster vomited lava over its other front leg, then moved to its back legs. Jedik-ikik warriors looked into the black eyes of death. To their credit, only a few jumped off the giant monster's legs.

The final Jedik-ikik, stubborn and brave, had formed a ring around the Zree's thigh. They stabbed it over and over. The monster roared in great pain. Its horrible face shot down at the Jedik-ikik. With a final quaking blast, the leg broke apart. Jedik-ikik soldiers fell to happy deaths, knowing they had made a difference in the war as the mountain fell on top of them.

9

While the Zree fell down, the other two Rentok stabbed inward into the vast city. K'tang pushed to the dome, the thing that gave him so much grief, while Renslot moved along the edge of the city, first toppling over the military tower and the general in his perch. After pounding into dust the ancient military compound (and the automaton that the astronauts had interviewed), mighty Renslot moved into the housing district, stomping on the historic district and trampling artifacts and regular citizens together. Renslot had no mercy for women, children, or the elderly. He did not weigh the balance of life in his hands. He did not care about good or evil, of promise-keepers or oath-breakers. Death was his only judgement, and he doled out judgement to all.

To the Rentok the soldiers ran. Each step of the Rentok was like a hundred steps for a Jedik-ikik warrior. Still, they ran back into their city. Some caught on to Renslot's tail. Others latched onto his legs. As they had trained, they climbed higher and higher. The life of their families and the future of their civilization depended on climbing higher. As the giant monster moved, wind currents formed around his body, carrying soldiers out into the open air to fall to New Death.

"Cleek!" the sergeants urged their soldiers. "Cleek rae tip!"

The destination was the strange mountain peaks that had cast shadows over the city for thousands of years. It would take a lot of soldiers to stop Renslot, more than they had. All that the soldiers in formation could do was wait. The pheromone command had not been given.

Then, a giant eruption from the center of the city bolted over the ancient remains. A projectile blazed across the sky. Renslot was too quick, though. For such a monstrous mountain, he ducked under the blast. The projectile hurtled into the atmosphere.

Now Renslot had a new target. The creature roared its rage and stomped across the city. He smashed his way through libraries and temples. All around, the undead died.

Up to his back, the warriors climbed. On his back, the Jedik-ikik waited.

Renslot stopped at the dome long enough to try to figure out the quickest way to destroy it. He pushed into the dome's great walls. He was like a monstrous, rocky dinosaur trying to re-enter his giant egg. The honeycomb structure of the beams was too strong for him to easily tear apart. It wouldn't give.

Inside, Jedik-ikik worked furiously to reload their weapon. When the monster went silent, they looked up from their work. The eyes of death watched them moving. When they stopped, it reached down into the dome and smashed the inside structure. Renslot curled his hand around five Jedik-ikik engineers and squeezed until their heads popped off and their insides were squishy in his hands.

Renslot roared his victory. It sounded like the gates of hell being opened.

For the Jedik-ikik soldiers on his spines, they finally received the pheromone signal. Rings of soldiers stabbed at Renslot's spines. Others slammed their spears into his legs, and another set, into his tail.

Renslot growled angrily at the mean little monsters eating away at his rocky flesh. One of the Jedik-ikik had the misfortune of being able to see the monster's glare. It was enough to make him stop. The look in the creature's eye told the Jedik-ikik more than any chart, philosophy, or training regimen. It was like living all your life singing God's graces, only to suddenly learn that God hated you. The Jedik-ikik dropped his spear and ran down the ridges of the mountain god. When his sergeant tried to stop him, he killed the sergeant and kept running.

Renslot shuddered and lowered his body. He closed his eyes and concentrated. Suddenly, the Jedik-ikik felt the heat rising up out of the rock. The heat became more and more intense. Light flared out of the ridges and rocky crevices along his back. When the light disappeared, there was nothing left of the Jedik-ikik except their shadows on his spine.

Renslot shoved his arms deep into the dome and pushed, reaching for the weapon's pivot point.

10

K'tang never made it to the dome. The creature got caught in the center of town, showering lightning on the troops of Ximortikrim. K'tang took to battling the army head-on. The army was eager to face him after all he had done. After all, K'tang was the first to awaken and the first to attack Ximortikrim.

Thousands of soldiers ran up and down his body while the giant monster did everything possible to destroy them. He breathed lightning all along his body, frying the undead. He swept his long arms around him, and like scythes, they cut down the soldiers where they stood.

The monster could feel his body being blown apart. It was like being stabbed a hundred thousand times by tiny little fireworks all over his rock-sheltered skin. He needed to do something quickly, but his lightning was weakening. The creature pulled one last bolt out of his chest. The forest of electricity grew around him, spreading to destroy everything within 30 meters around him.

The Jedik-ikik soldiers were eviscerated, but not without exacting their own price. K'tang lay prostrate on his knees, his long arms at his side like the long draws of a lonely mountain. Smoke wafted in the dark clouds around him.

Up ahead of him, a great redness poured out from under the dome. Renslot watched as lava flamed along the aqueduct system, rising along the tracks on its way to the center fields where the dead lay with K'tang. K'tang barely had time to lift his arms in protest as lava flooded over him. Higher arches dropped water on top of the lava-coated monster. Rock exploded and water steamed instantly. The giant rock monster fought back helplessly against the geologic weapons, slinging burning globs of lava into buildings as he tried to stand up.

Renslot shoved his hands into the lava in an attempt to destroy the aqueduct. The heat was too intense for the monster. He recoiled.

Back in the fields of battle, the lava and the water were too much for K'tang. The lava solidified under the pressure of the cooling water, slowly freezing the mountain god into place. Jedik-ikik cheered, and the lava and water stopped flowing. Renslot and the lava monster, lacking one less leg, retreated back toward the mountains.

CHAPTER FIVE: EMILY'S PLAN

1

"Wait. They're coming here!" Cole realized. "Those monsters, they're coming this way."

"There's no guarantee they're coming here," Emily said. "They may just be going back to the mountains."

"What if they're not? Can we take that chance? We're on the other side of those mountains."

Emily thought of their training. Part of adapting to new challenges was being able to see the next challenge and analyze it before taking it on. She had to agree with her husband.

While Emily contemplated their next move, Mathieu said, "There's no way they should be able to walk either. Hear me out. Those things have to be what, at least five hundred thousand tons? That's impossible to lift, hey."

"We have five of the brightest minds on any planet sitting right here in this room," Emily said. (C.C. had returned to the main room during the battle.) "For three years, we trained for every kind of eventuality that NASA could throw at us, so if there is anyone who can figure this out, we are the ones to do it. First, though, we have to figure out what we're up against, so I want all the data we have on these things now. We're going to make the implausible plausible."

Anna stepped forward. "They share a mix of properties from both animals and plants. Last night while I was analyzing our data, I was watching some of the recordings. The way they had to pull themselves free of the ground, it's like they had a root system and were feeding off the energy from the ground. In fact, I think they are smaller than they appear now. They're just covered in a few thousand years of dirt and foliage. Remember that patch of skin we found under the rock?"

C.C. said, "There's more." He opened up a graphics file on the table monitor. "This should look familiar. It is the topographical view of the area, showing the Calvary Mountains near Ximortikrim." He pressed a few buttons. The mountains and the valley were laid out in bright hues. "This is a geological map. It shows the relatively useless rock below the surface, though there were trace iron elements. We didn't dig any deeper, no pun intended. Well, now I have." He brought up a more detailed examination of the mountains. They couldn't be clearer.

"Those look like skeletons," Cole said.

"Those aren't mountains. They're graves," Emily said.

"Have you ever looked at a mountain and thought it looked like someone sleeping? In this case, it really was happening," C.C. said. "But there's more. See, this spectral imaging pushes out biological 'noise.' The program assumed the biomass was more rock. This imaging shows a mix of iron and titanium and a metal I haven't seen before. These aren't bone skeletons. They're metal. I think that sound we hear every time one stands up-that metal banging sound."

"Tok, tok, tok," Cole said.

"Right. That must be gears of something in the skeleton moving. Kind of like they are turning on."

"There's no way they should be able to walk," Mathieu said. "I stand by what I said earlier. It is a physical impossibility, alien matter or not."

"Who cares?" Cole interjected. "We need to be figuring out how to destroy these things, not how they can stand."

"But if we can understand how they move, then we can use that to our advantage," Emily said.

Anna said, "Right. So instead of assuming that they are all granite, assume that at least half of what we see is biomass, and the weight comes down to more like a hundred thousand tons. That weight will go down more depending on how much is biomass and how much of the rock is sedentary instead of granite."

"With the metal skeleton, that must be what's offsetting the density of the monster's biomass." Seeing the confusion in the eyes of Emily's husband, C.C. said, "Let me give the quick tour of what we're talking about. It's impossible to weigh the giant monster, but we can make some assumptions based on its density. We can use water displacement to help us here. This is the old story of Archimedes and how he needed to figure out whether some silver had been used in the forging of his king's crown. He noticed that when he got into a tub, the water rose, and he realized this same effect could determine the volume of the crown."

"And he ran through the streets naked crying out eureka!" Anna added excitedly.

"Exactly," C.C. said. "Now, we could 3D print a model of the Rentok based on our imagery and then dunk the model in a tank of water, but we

don't have the time, so we're making assumptions on the displacement."
He took out a dry erase marker and wrote on the table:

.375m

2.9 l

"That's the height of a hypothetical 'Rentok' model and its relative water displacement."

"So you're making this up," Cole said

"Hypothetical. That's different."

"How? I'm not going to argue. Go ahead. Finish."

"Eyeballing the big guy, I'm guessing he's 500 meters high. If I take that number, and I divide it by my model, I get 1.7 million. Take that and my displacement, and then multiply by density of 2.75 which is the relative density of granite, that tells me that the thing ways 14.2 million kilograms or about 500 tons."

Anna drew an x through 2.75 and wrote in green beside it ".9." "That's the relative density of a crocodile." She wrote a few other problems and circled "103K tons." She said, "Cole, that's the relative tonnage of the creature if it is half biomass and half granite."

"So what do we do with that?"

"Newton," Emily said. "An object in motion tends to stay in motion."

"Should we launch it into space with our collected fuel?" Mathieu asked.

"That's risky, and I don't think there's enough fuel to launch it into space, but that's a good idea. No, I was thinking that in this weak gravity, we could trip it. Once it goes down, then we will have the advantage."

"Trip it?" Cole asked. "Seriously? I love you, babe, but we don't have any 1000-foot-long trip wires that I know of."

Emily smiled. Cole was not encouraged.

2

Mathieu and C.C. were fitting the seismic pulse cannons onto the DSMUs when Emily walked over.

"You've got to hurry. I estimate the Rentok will be here in five minutes."

"I'm doing everything I can, Emily," Mathieu said. He squinted at a small keyboard and monitor clipped into the DSMU's shell. "I'm having to code the pulse cannons into the DSMUs, and I keep running into errors. We're fortunate that everything NASA made came with universal adapters. It's like one giant Lego set. But that doesn't mean the parts want to play together. Not to mention that while I'm doing this the fokken ground won't stop shaking."

"Don't let me stop you."

C.C. followed Emily as she walked toward the Ascent Vehicle. "This is a crazy stunt, you know."

"It is the application of basic physical principles."

"Right. In ways that they've never been tested before. You'll be lucky you don't destroy the Hab and all of Ximortikrim."

"There is the potential energy output not unlike an atom bomb," she said. "It's risky, but if you have another option, I'm all ears. Make it quick, though." She checked her timer. "Four minutes until the big bad arrives."

C.C. grabbed her by the elbow. She tore out of it.

"We have history together. You can't walk off on me."

"I'm the commander. I can walk off on anybody I want."

"Emily, I want you to know that I still plan to take over as commander. Once the Rentok are destroyed, this mission belongs to me."

3

BOOM
BOOM
BOOM

REEEEE-AA-RGH!

The sound filled their helmets. Cole cringed.

"I don't like this plan," he told his crewmates.

"You wouldn't have liked any plan," Mathieu said. "Relax. All you have to do is drive a car. The rest is on us."

"I've only driven this car once."

C.C. said, "And you didn't crash it, unlike the EDL simulator, so how bad can it be?"

"I'm bait." His words were punctuated with the quaking sound of the Rentok.

"There is that."

"My wife made me bait."

"I love you," she said beseechingly. "Come on. It's the safest place for you, honey."

"Hey, it's here," Anna said.

Mathieu said a little prayer. "Holy Mary, look after us." He made the sign of the cross. "Now and at the hour of our death."

"That's uplifting," C.C. said.

"Let's science this SOB into the Stone Age," Emily said. "How about that?"

"Much better."

"Cole, go!"

Behind him, he saw the two giant Rentok, creatures much bigger than any animal he'd ever seen in his life. The Rentok they did not know were named Zree and Renslot, and they were coming over the final mountain. A mountain, Cole reminded himself, that they had only recently learned was a giant burial mound.

Cole pushed the gear stick forward and shoved his boot down on the accelerator. The giant rover lurched forward. Its cabin bucked backward in complaint, as if he'd just hit something.

"Slow down, Earnhardt," Mathieu said. "That's not a sports car you're driving."

"Right." He lifted his foot and exhaled slowly. The Golgotha Exploration Activity Rover, or GEAR, pushed across the clearing. Cole turned on his rearview mirror. It showed nothing but jungle. He adjusted the angle. He saw trees, then boulders, then legs, a body, and finally, a head covered in deep crevices. Some of those crevices ended in eyeholes and nostrils and a large, gaping mouth full of flaming colors.

He hit the lights, and the metal Christmas tree bolted to the solar panel railings lit up all red and green and yellow and blue. A string of lights that read "Merry Christmas" shined in the morning light. It even had a big, yellow star perched on top that had Burt Ives singing "Holly Jolly Christmas."

"Personally, I would've preferred Brenda Lee," Anna said. She sang out, "Rocking around the Christmas tree, at the Christmas party hop."

"You be bait, you get to pick the song," Cole said.

In the rear view camera, the giant magma monster's eyes turned to Cole. He pressed down on the accelerator.

"Time to get gone," he said. The GEAR pushed up to 19 kilometers per hour. It maxed out at 20, but Mathieu had been more than happy to bypass those securities for Cole. Now, the GEAR could do a whopping 30 kilometers per hour.

All eight wheels of the GEAR dug into the sand as the rover sped across the field and away to the next closest mountain.

"Hurry up, baby," Emily said. "Remember, we don't want them anywhere near the Hab."

"Yes, ma'am."

The GEAR threw dirt in giant waves around it. In the low gravity, they didn't immediately fall back to the ground, at least not by Earth standards. They kind of hung in the air like deflated helium balloons.

As he fled to the southern mountain, two giant monsters on his tail, he discovered that he was paying more attention to the monsters than he was to what was in front of him. The GEAR hit a rock and bounced into the air. It bounced about three times higher than it would have bounced on Earth, which was almost half a meter of air between the GEAR and the ground. He landed with a crashing thud, spewing dirt. Cole nearly overcompensated for the rover's trajectory and flipped it on its side. Fortunately, the last bit of gravity was working, and pulled the right-side tires back to the ground.

"Careful," Emily said.

Mathieu laughed. "That looked awesome, Cole! I'm sure that was some kind of off-roading record. Did you see how much air you caught? People back home are going to be thinking you did that deliberately."

"Not once they get to know him," C.C. said.

"You'll have to show me if I survive this. This thing drives with all the agility of a dumpster truck."

"You'll survive," Emily said. "But you have to go faster, baby. They're gaining on you."

He had lost time while airborne and steering out of the bounce. The GEAR spun around a bit. It was precious time that the giant Rentok needed to catch up to him. The faster Zree tried to stomp on the GEAR but missed by a few meters. The impact, though, was enough to bounce the GEAR around some more. Cole said a little prayer of thanks that the rover did not go up into the air a second time.

"Faster!" Emily encouraged him.

"I'm going as fast as I can," Cole said.

"You're not going thirty," Mathieu countered. "Push harder."

"I don't know what to tell you, Mathieu. My foot is on the floor."

Renslot reached for the Christmas tree with its massive arms. A tidal wave of rock swept at the GEAR. As Cole saw through the rearview monitor the wall of rock come flying at him, he thought of his wife and the nephew he'd never met. "Mellifluous," he said.

The GEAR jounced forward as the wall swept behind him. His front wheels went up, and suddenly he found himself climbing up the second mountain.

"I made it!"

The GEAR climbed up the low bank. The monsters followed. When he finally came over the steep rise, he was nearly launched into the air again. It certainly felt like it to Cole. All he could see in front of him was the blue horizon and the clouds. Then the nose of the GEAR dipped down, and it slammed into the rock beneath it. He was looking almost down at the tree line.

"Veer left!" his wife shouted at him. He veered.

Over the ridge rose the two monstrous heads.

"Holy shit, they're big," C.C. said.

The giant dinosaurian rock monster, the one the Jedik-ikik called Renslot, came over the ridge first. He took two steps and was almost to the bottom. Then came the volcano monster. As soon as it took its first step onto the ridge, Emily shouted, "NOW!"

Four NASA bulldozers, repurposed from forest clearing, powered by robots, steamrolled into the monster's feet while the rest of the robots jumped out from behind trees and pushed into the monster.

"I hope this works," C.C. said.

"It will," Emily said. "It's just math."

Mathieu, C.C., and Anna spark-started their SRBs and launched into the back of the walking death. They slammed into it with the power of three Saturn Rockets. They got exactly what they had hoped for. Caught off guard, the three-legged monster fell forward. It collided with the even bigger rock monster, and they both slammed into the ground.

THOOM

The rocket-powered DSMUs steered away from the destruction. A giant wave of dirt and rocks shot out from the monsters. A massive geological tsunami rippled across the valley and slammed into the southern mountain. The ripple went right up to the edge of the ridge, but it did not splash over.

As Cole retreated back toward the Hab, an enormous cloud of dirt flowed over him. One minute he could see fine, and the next, he was enveloped in total darkness, long fingers of dust and dirt reaching around him. The wind from the collision buffeted the GEAR. First it shuddered, and then it tipped. Without any visibility, he couldn't actually see himself being flung into the air. He felt weightless, and then he was tumbling and rolling. The windows shattered in the GEAR. Thankfully, he was belted in, but that did nothing to defend him against the rocks that came crashing through the broken windows and into his helmet.

Cole knew he was dead. No amount of training could prevent his death. His life was dependent on the will of inertia. He thought to hail his wife one last time, but he couldn't find any of the keys. The air was full of brown and black dust blowing everywhere, and the GEAR was tumbling like palm trees in a hurricane. The last thing he thought of before losing consciousness was his wife and his nephew. He hoped she'd remember him, but go on and make a good life with the remainder of her years. He knew she would raise Story as her own. She'd be the best damn aunt Story could've ever had, and she'd do everything to raise him right.

But most of all, he hoped she'd kill every last one of those monsters.

4

Screaming woke him up. Screaming, and the low oxygen alarm going off in his suit.

The screaming, he knew, was his friends. The alarm was a little thing called the "suit impact alarm." It meant his AXES suit was open and he was breathing in carbon monoxide. He was lucky that he hadn't slipped into oblivion while he was unconscious.

His view of the outside world was restricted by the rover. He was mostly upside down, one set of wheels laying in the dirt, the other set sprawled in the air. The GEAR blared its own alarms. System failures, low oxygen alerts, and of course, more impact alarms.

"Shut up," he growled at the alarms. His words came out slurred. The alarms were doing nothing for the massive headache that was growing inside his skull. He put his hands to his head. No bleeding. At least there was that.

"Cole?" Emily shouted into his comm. "I thought you were dead."

"Maybe I am. Hang on. I've got to get to a helmet first." He unstrapped his five-point buckle and fell to the GEAR's ceiling, rolling onto his shoulder as much as possible to reduce the damage.

"Go on. Get out of here," he heard C.C. say to somebody, clearly not him.

Cole slowly pulled himself up. His whole body ached, like he'd spent the last ten hours in a Soyuz landing simulator. He staggered to the back of the GEAR, shutting off alarms as he went. Yes, he knew an impact had happened. Yes, he knew the environmental system was compromised. Yes, yes, yes. Now shut the hell up. His brain felt two sizes too big for his skull.

The GEAR stowed two emergency AXES suits on racks in the back of the GEAR. Both were in fine condition...except for the helmets, which were pulverized.

"You've got to be kidding me," Cole said, and then he slumped in the corner. Breathing without coughing was hard. Concentrating was even harder.

"What's wrong, Cole? Did you get to the AXES suits in the back of the GEAR?" Emily asked.

"I did, but their helmets are broken, too."

"You've got to look for another helmet, Cole. Maybe somebody left one there. If there isn't another helmet, you've got to find some other way to insulate yourself from the carbon monoxide. It will kill you."

"I know," he said, with a little laugh. "I'm so tired, though, Emily."

"Don't give up, Cole."

"I'm not giving up. I'm just resting."

There was more chaos in his eardrums. He didn't know who was shouting at the others. He also wasn't sure if the pounding in his head was just his headache on steroids, or if the monsters were back up on their feet.

"Baby, get up. I love you. Get up."

"I...don't think I can," he mumbled. He was thinking of their training and how fortunate he'd been to be able to travel with his wife. Everybody says they want to travel, but how many of them actually go anywhere? Well, 51 Golgotha was definitely more travel than any of the other couples they knew (expect the Sorensons. Becky and Greg had traveled to two planets already before he ever met them). They were blowhards, he thought. Screw them.

Butler was the xeno-linguist assigned to the mission. He was a good fit, too. He was about Cole's age, and one of the best linguists in the world. He was out of Northwestern. Of the five people brought in to decipher the language of the Jedik-ikik, Cole and Leo were two of them. But Leo broke three vertebras in the car accident, so NASA came to Cole to fill his role. He might not have been the adventurer his wife was, but he was no agoraphobe, either. He passed the physical exams and got to spend the next three months in a crash course to learn and practice as much of the systems as possible. It was exhilarating being on the other side of those rooms. He'd been the one training astronauts how to work the Jedik-ikik language before NASA added Leo to the roster. Now he was the astronaut learning from the trainers.

He liked those memories, and he liked that dream. It was a good dream to die in, if that was what fate had in store for him.

"You're not dying on Emily, man," a voice said from somewhere beyond the darkness. Cole looked for it in the dark but could not find it.

"Breathe in," the voice said again. *What is breathing?* Cole asked in his mind. He wasn't sure if the voice heard him. He wasn't sure of anything anymore.

"Come on. Em is gonna kill me if you don't open your eyes up right now," the voice said. He was sure the voice belonged to C.C. He wasn't sure he ever really liked C.C. There always seemed to be an unspoken competition between the two of them, a competition seeded in her love for Cole and his life-long friendship with C.C. He knew it was him, though. Nobody else called her "Em."

Suddenly, his lungs kicked in on him. He felt better almost immediately, but he was still dizzy. His eyes fluttered open like a newborn. C.C. didn't smile per se, but he didn't look disappointed either.

Cole glanced around. He wore a new AXES suit. C.C. did not. Was he holding his breath?

"You need this more than me," Cole said.

"No. I can sustain myself off of the DSMU's filtration system. I just wanted to make sure you weren't brain dead."

Cole held his hands out like a magician finishing an amazing trick: *Ta-da! Alive!*

C.C. patted him on the shoulder, then climbed back into the DSMU and closed the hatch. A few dozen eye holes brightened with life on top of the hatch, and then the filtration tube breathed a gasp as it shunted the poisonous gases back into the atmosphere.

"You ready, Cole?"

"Ready for what?"

"Not dying was the easy part. We've got to catch up to everyone else. Catch up to those things."

5

The monster called Zree fell forward coming over the side of the mountain. The monster crashed into Renslot, who fell down, too. Renslot fell face forward into the ground, and Zree tumbled onto his back. The combined fall of the two giants caused dirt and rock to explode everywhere. As planned, the DSMUs veered away from the explosion. The robots were not so lucky. They were all but destroyed in the collision.

Elsewhere, the GEAR was throttled by the ground tsunami, and Cole gave his life over to inertia.

Before the dust could settle, Anna, Mathieu, and C.C. dove back into the cloud. They landed on Zree and began hitting him with their seismic pulse cannons. They gave no more than three pulse blasts in a spot before moving to a new spot.

Beneath them, the monster railed. Giant wedges of rock—the creature's arms and legs—whooshed above them as the monster worked to gain purchase and upright itself. The astronauts had planned on the creature's movements, so they stayed on its chest.

Mathieu's eyes were messing with him. Everything was a blur. He followed the blur of his friends into battle, and now he was avoiding the blur of the giant monster's arms. He hoped he was drilling in the right place. Felt confident about his odds. He was pretty good, spatially, even without perfect vision.

"I went too deep!" Anna said. From under her, a jet of hot air shot up and over her mech suit. Bright red lava bubbled from the hole she shot in the Zree's surface.

"Keep moving," C.C. said. "The goal is to destabilize the magma inside and cause a catastrophic eruption."

The Rentok bucked underneath them, hoping to knock them off his rocky surface, but the astronauts were using tethers shot into the rock to keep them strapped to the creature.

The monster roared.

"He's going to either stand up or come after us," C.C. said. "Everybody ready?"

"As ready as we're going to be," Mathieu said.

Gargantuan arms rammed at them. The astronauts barely jumped in time, falling into crevices in the creature's chest. Giant fingers scratched at the crevices.

Mathieu cried out. He'd been caught. The fingers snatched him and flung him into the dust.

"Mathieu, you okay?" When Mathieu didn't respond, C.C. called out for him again. "Mathieu!"

"I'm alright," he finally said. "Just a little banged up."

"We will rendezvous to your GPS location once we've destroyed the beasts."

But then the creature began to rise.

"Hold on!" C.C. shouted. "We're almost there."

As Zree stood up, he rose above the settling dust. C.C. could make out Anna. She was at her last point, and so was he. Only two more points needed to be blasted before they could trigger the eruption. They were making excellent progress.

"I'll take care of those last two holes. You get out of here," C.C. said.

"Nonsense. Somebody has to trigger Mount Monstersaurus to erupt. It will be quicker if I do it."

He couldn't argue with that. As Anna moved toward the center of the monster's chest, C.C. used the tethering system to move to Mathieu's last holes.

A deadly roar deafened their ears. It seemed to come from nowhere, though the astronauts knew exactly where it came from. The largest of the monsters was getting back up.

The dinosaurian head ascended slowly through the dust cloud like a rock outcropping in the fog. Two red eyes glared at C.C. and Anna as the giant monster continued moving upward. Its gaze never left the astronauts as it stood up.

"We need to leave now," Anna said.

"Go on. Get out of here," C.C. said. "I'll finish this."

"Don't be a martyr. You don't have the genes for it."

"Good point."

"Time for Plan B."

6

C.C. landed near the GEAR. It was half-buried in the dust and looked a hell of a lot worse than he thought Cole was capable of withstanding.

"You still in there?"

Cole didn't respond.

Out on the plains, the two monsters moved toward the Hab, which made an easy target out in the open. Anna and Mathieu followed them at a safe distance.

"You don't have to do this, Em," C.C. said. "We can find another way."

"One way or another, the Hab's going down today," she shot back.

"That is the only link to the Anchor. If you destroy it..."

"If I destroy it, we can figure out what to do after that." Emily spoke with a tone of finality. "Get my husband."

"Let her work," Anna said.

C.C. ripped back the sides of the GEAR. Lying among the suits in the back of the rover, he saw Cole deep in sleep, like Cinderella waiting for her prince to come. C.C. knew he didn't have any extra gear in the DSMUs, so he removed his AXES helmet and climbed out of the embryonic-like safety of his DSMU and secured his helmet onto Cole's AXES suit. The suit pressurized, then began purging the suit of carbon monoxide while converting the outside air into oxygen.

Once C.C. confirmed that Cole was alive, and after he placed him in the DSMU, he climbed back into the DSMU and exhaled. He knew he'd be okay. He'd learned to hold his breath for two minutes during their training, which prepared them for aborted ascent scenarios that had them landing in the middle of the Pacific Ocean. They had to pick up scuba diving lessons and learn open ocean wilderness survival, up to and including holding their breath for at least one minute. C.C. was okay. Loads better than Cole, who had held his breath one time for one minute. Emily was the champion, though. She could hold her breath for three minutes and twenty eight seconds.

He held Cole in his arms and entered the "Run" program into the DSMU's command system. He was tired of burning SRBs. The DSMU was no Jesse Owens when it came to speed, but it wasn't a couch potato either. Twenty four kilometers an hour—the speed of the GEAR when its limitations weren't disengaged, by the way—was the top speed of a running DSMU. He aimed for the monsters and decided to put the speedometer to the test.

No matter what speed he set, though, the monsters were too far away for him to catch up. They would be at the Hab before him. And then, whatever happened, he'd have no control over it.

"I've been thinking," he said. "Maybe there is another way of doing this."

"Oh?" Emily asked.

7

Emily watched her husband go streaking across the plains in the GEAR with the Christmas lights flashing on top. She giggled to herself. Then the colossal thundering of the giant monsters whammed everywhere. The two monsters chased her husband across the plains, and her husband bounced around as he fled.

She wondered about the plains. They were known only as Plains 421. *Colossal plains? Cole's Plains? That had a much better ring to it.* And he'd earned it, hadn't he? Certainly naming things was one of the perks of being the first person to set place somewhere, a sort of spoils of war for explorers. He'd probably tease her about naming something *plain* after him, of course, but he'd see the sincerity in the gesture. He'd love her for it, too. That was how they were. So different, and yet so the same.

The monsters went over the southern mountain. *Again, we really need to name these places*, she thought. That was Mountain 421, to correspond with Plains 421.

Emily tensed up. This was the pivotal moment. She trusted her math, but that didn't mean she wasn't still a little nervous about the trap. What if something went wrong? What if the bulldozers were too slow for the monsters, or if the DSMUs didn't hit them quite the way they should, making her thrust equations too low to topple the two great behemoths? She could easily think of a dozen or two things that could go wrong. She hoped everything would go right.

The three-legged monster tripped and fell over the goliath, and they hit the ground with a crash that rocked her in the Ascent Vehicle. A giant dust cloud blew across the mountain and then subsided.

Once the world stopped swaying back and forth, she began making the lift adjustments. The ascent vehicle was tilted ten degrees to the south for launch purposes. That would not do. The support beams repositioned the ascent vehicle based on her inputs. She felt the vehicle strain against the support beams. It was now almost thirty degrees to the east. Any steeper of a tilt, and she risked falling backwards onto the ground and exploding. No biggie.

She checked her LOX fuel. Reserves were 99%. She was good. She turned off the automated countdown clocks. The warning alarms blared. She shut them off, too. They were just doing her job, but she knew what she was doing.

She was now looking back over 51 Golgotha upside down, as if the sky was the ground, and a strange, rocky terrain loomed over it.

She breathed in and out slowly and tried to relax.

Two giant heads appeared in her window view. Erupting the monster had failed. They were moving toward her now, as expected. There was something strange about the two giant monsters that they hadn't figured out yet (as was pretty much everything they hadn't accounted for—there were twenty eight things on her list of unaccounted items for the giant monsters). The monsters had stared at the graves of the other fallen monsters. Were they thinking about them? Were they grieving lost family or friends? Or was there something more to it? She had a hunch it wasn't grief. The way they stood around staring at the graves. It reminded her of radio towers, just standing there lifeless. These monsters were on to more than they let on. They weren't dumb brutes wracking vengeance for nature. Either they were keenly aware, or they were under somebody's control. Either way, Emily figured they would recognize the threat of the Hab and go for it if they were not destroyed in the fall.

This was Plan B, a.k.a., the Final Solution, a.k.a., Emily Is Off Her Gourd.

She synced up the Ascent Vehicle's computer, Major Main 101, with OGRA. Then she turned off the Abort locks. These were preset destinations that would send the Ascent Vehicle to specific landing spots should the mission need to be aborted. Of course, she had no intention of aborting the takeoff.

As the earth shook and the monsters marched across the plains toward her, she continued her flight preparations, shutting down emergency systems and purging the main engines and pressurizing the LOX tanks.

"Commander Emily Musgrove," OGRA said. "I must again request that you do not use the Ascent Vehicle for any purpose other than return to the Anchor."

"Thank you, OGRA. I understand, but our lives are threatened. This is the only way to stop the monsters from killing us."

"You know this is all being recorded and returned to Earth?"

"Yes."

"Then may I quote to you from the launch of STS-1?"

"Yes, OGRA."

"If you will accept my edits, 'You go forward this morning in a daring enterprise, carrying the hopes and dreams of all the people of Earth with you.'"

"Thank you, OGRA."

"You don't have to do this, Em," C.C. said. "We can find another way."

"One way or another, the Hab's going down today," Emily said. She was looking at the approaching monsters carrying the power of mass destruction with them.

"That is the only link to the Anchor. If you destroy it..."

"If I destroy it, we can figure out what to do after that. Get my husband."

"Let her work," Anna said.

She maneuvered around the guidance system in Main Major 101, convincing it that her manual adjustments would not need to be overridden.

"I've been thinking," C.C. said. "Maybe there is another way of doing this."

"Oh?" Emily asked. "What'd you have in mind?"

"What if we blew up the ISRU Station? OGRA could do that pretty easily, couldn't you, OGRA?"

"I am not authorized to detonate," OGRA said.

"But we could authorize you."

The monsters were within a few hundred yards of the Ascent Vehicle.

"Thank you, C.C., but I think we've run out of options," Emily said.

"No, there are more. You shouldn't be doing this."

"I'm the commander and it was my plan. I am exactly the person to do this."

"C.C., stop," Anna said. "Please, just stop. Let her go in peace."

"But I'm not ready to let her go. I'm not ready to let any of this go."

"You are the bravest woman I know," Mathieu said. "Dankie, Emily. Saam met God, my suster."

"I will see you all soon," Emily said. The largest monster, the one with all the teeth and the spines, reached out for the Ascent Vehicle. Emily pressed the launch button. Sparks fired, and the vehicle spewed LOX. Emily throttled down, and the Ascent Vehicle exploded into the monsters. The monsters shrieked. Covered in fire, they staggered backwards away from the launch complex.

8

The sound of the Ascent Vehicle's engines firing was so intense, it woke Cole from his slumber. He looked across the plains and saw the Ascent Vehicle taking off in a plume of fire and smoke.

"Noooo!" Cole shouted. He nearly squirmed out of the arms of C.C.'s DSMU.

9

Emily had never been kicked in the guts so hard she felt her intestines have an out-of-body experience. She tried to figure out what was happening, but her screen had gone dark. Whatever happened, she was going to do it blind.

Without sight, all she could rely on was her hearing, but it was hard to discern anything through the cacophony playing out around her. Alarms blared, things bumped around in the cockpit, and her heart was thudding in her chest louder than the rest combined. It was like a big bass drum keeping time for the ensuing disaster. Through it all, though, she distinctly heard the monsters roaring, and then suddenly three explosions in quick successions. Bmpf! Bmpf! Bmpf!

The Crew Escape Vehicle was hurtling away from the collision like a piece of debris in an auto accident, tumbling over and over while red hot. The Abort System emergency overrides (different from the Abort locks) blared at her while the Control Compromise Engines flared outward. Within seconds they had performed a minor miracle and stabilized the CEV in mid-air. Slowly, the CEV descended to the ground.

Emily had only commanded space missions twice before, and she'd *never* had to use the CEV. While overly grateful for the system that saved her life, she wasn't sure she'd ever try that again. Her insides felt like jelly, like somehow in all the tumbling, her intestines had wrapped around her lungs, and her heart was flung under her stomach. Everything was out of sorts.

"How are you, Commander Emily Musgrove?" OGRA asked.

She knew the question was purely perfunctory. OGRA had the readings of all of Emily's vitals and a bunch of less-than-vital, too. OGRA knew better than Emily how she was doing. Still, Emily said, "Other than my guts having an out-of-body experience, I think I'm fine."

Emily unbuckled and slowly opened the CEV's door. She stood on the ladder and scanned for the monsters. They were retreating back to the graves from where they came. She was a little disappointed. She'd hoped the monsters would be torn to pieces by her last-ditch effort. Yet somehow, they survived.

CHAPTER SIX: FAULT TREE ANALYSIS

1

"Do we go after them?" Mathieu asked. "They aren't that far."

"You must be joking," Cole said. "Emily, are you there? Come in."

Using the sights on their suits, they could see the Ascent Vehicle standing erect on the plains. Emily stood in the open cockpit door.

"She's about six clicks from us," C.C. said.

"Why doesn't she answer? Were her mics broken?"

"Possibly," C.C. replied.

"I need to go to her."

"She's at least a half hour's run from us in a DSMU that's fully charged. She'll catch up to us."

"Screw that. She's my wife. I am going to go see my wife. You can do whatever the hell you want."

C.C. sighed. "Okay. Take my DSMU. Everybody else, we've got some cleaning up to do."

"What about the Mega Xenon?" Anna asked.

"That's a nice word for it. I like it," C.C. said. "We're going after the Mega Xenons once we do a bit of recovery and work out a strategy for killing or containing them."

2

The DSMU ran full throttle across the plains, kicking up dust as it ran. On his screens, Cole saw his wife's DSMU running toward him. Both DSMUs stopped abruptly in front of each other. The husband and wife climbed out of the mechs as quickly as possible and ran into each other's arms. Emily had tears down her face as they held each other tightly.

"I thought," he started to say, but then she put her hands on his face and pressed her lips hard against his. She held him there for what felt like a lifetime to her. He did not mind. He did not want to lose her again.

As their arms moved across their bodies and they hugged each other tightly, he said, "I thought you were dead. I didn't see the CEV escape. I thought everything went up."

"I'm sorry. I won't do that again."

"You better not. I think I aged thirty years over there. I was so scared."

"I know. I'm sorry. I had to, though."

"I know. It was your plan. All of it. Including the backup plan. Why couldn't I be the person to do the backup plan?"

"You don't know all the sequences backwards and forwards and how to shut them down."

"I know. But I would have felt better being the one doing it."

"I wouldn't have felt better."

"I'm just so glad you're alive. Don't pull another stunt like that again."

"I won't."

Cole knew differently. This was the woman who rappelled off of Olympus Mons on a dare. NASA was not happy with that stunt, and neither was Cole, but she did it anyway. It nearly cost her the command of this mission (NASA called her "controversial" during her interview, and it had been widely rumored that Kirk Bearcousins would have received the command had she not argued passionately with the center director for the position). Cole had resigned himself long ago to the idea of being married to a woman as likely to jump off the top rail as she was to take the stairs.

"But maybe it's time to really mean it. We're out here on a distant planet where every minute something's trying to kill us, whether it's undead aliens or giant monsters or the inherent environment itself. So maybe it's time to accept the high likelihood of death and not compound the equation?" He thought if he put it in engineering terms, he could win her over.

"Or maybe we are already so many magnitudes of order higher in that percentage of likelihood of death, that any brash, crazy thing I do is insignificant in comparison to what is out there?" A smile twitched at the ends of her lips when she said it.

"Seriously, Emily? After all that, you're going to stand here and…"

"I'm just kidding."

"I'm not!" His cheeks were flushed with anger.

"I'm sorry." She brushed his arm up and down. "Let me make it up to you."

She was smiling again. At first he didn't understand what she was getting at, but when it finally did, he asked, "Out here?"

"Well, no. I can't hold my breath that long."

"This is really awkward," C.C. said over the comm. "Neither of you turned your channels off. You're fully mic'ed up."

"Please turn off your mic before going to the CEV," Mathieu said.

"I'm never going in the CEV," Anna said.

Emily's mouth was a giant "O" of surprise. She turned her channel off.

3

The three-legged, magma-spewing beast and the rock dragon limped to the open graves, where stone lay split open like eggs. The giant monsters searched the area, noses sniffing at their long-lost comrades. To the north, they gave a silent nod of regret to their fallen brother, melded under magma. A giant crowd of Jedik-ikik worked to break him open. They wanted to steal the secrets within the Rentok. The Jedik-ikik had out-survived the Rentok, so they would have their secrets soon enough. The Jedik-ikik stopped their buzzing and watched the two monsters warily. When the two giants moved away from the city, away from its broken walls, and away from the mountains, the Jedik-ikik returned to their victory.

The last two Rentok wandered to the west. Each footstep was a huge undertaking. Slower and slower they walked, until finally, the Rentok fell over. By then, they had entered a desert full of sand dunes. The wave of energy from their fall was big enough to reform the dunes in a three kilometer radius.

The wind blew.

4

Back at the Hab, Emily and Cole entered with a glow and a half-smile.

Mathieu whistled at them teasingly. Anna clapped.

"Knock it off," Emily said gently. Cole would have nothing of it. He took a bow.

"Don't get too proud," Emily said.

"You all were gone for at least two hours. I'm impressed," Mathieu said.

"Well, she was ready to go back, but I was like, 'Hey, I gotta impress Mathieu. He doesn't impress easily.'"

"Always glad to help."

"This is getting weird," Emily said. "Knock it off. Where's C.C.?"

"He is at the satellite station. It was damaged, and he was trying to send a message back to the Anchor."

"What kind of message, Mathieu?"

"He was just saying that we are all well."

"You're still a terrible liar, Mathieu. What is he really saying?"

Mathieu glanced at Anna. She shrugged.

"He's taking control of the team again, isn't he?"

"He says now that the two giant monsters are dead, the threat is over."

"And Ximortikrim?" Cole asked.

Their lack of an answer was all that Cole and Emily needed.

"You stay here," she ordered her husband. "This is commander business."

5

Of the three satellite dishes at the station, only one was still operating. One looked like a half-moon. The other had no more than a rind of the original dish.

Hands swinging, Emily took big steps toward C.C.

"How dare you?" she asked.

"It's not what you think," he said. "Turn off your comm. Please." He turned his off.

She turned hers off and spat out, "What do you mean, *not what I think*? According to every other Titan Space employee on this planet, you're phoning home to say that you're taking command of the mission."

He held his hands up. "I know. I know. And that's what I came out here to do. But I didn't do it."

C.C. set the wrench against a bolt that didn't need tweaking and tweaked it anyway. "You're reckless, and you're brash, and you're even a little derisive sometimes. And you don't see the world the way I do. I wish you did. I wish you could see its potential for commercialization. For jobs. For money in pockets of people who really need it."

"I see it, too."

"No, not really. You're an explorer, Emily. You always have been. All you see is the next mountain to climb, the next planet to visit. And I'm not saying there's anything wrong with that. I'm just saying that there has to be more to what we do than exploring. We can't always be in Palo Duro Canyon, looking for lizards and ghosts and lost mines. We gotta build something, too."

"So build. You don't need me."

"But I do, Em. I've always needed you."

Emily searched his eyes for something dangerous, something she didn't want to talk about.

"I'm not trying to dig up bones here, Em. The past is the past, especially when it's seven light years away."

"Then what is your goal here? What are you trying to accomplish with this conversation?"

C.C. sighed. Something was bugging him, and he was having a hard time getting it out.

Emily held his hand. "Earth to C.C., come in."

"I need to make a deal with you, here and now, that we are going to colonize 51 Golgotha."

"What? No."

"Listen to me first. Our goal is the colonization of planets with viable resources, resources Earth needs. Now, as soon as we set foot on the planet, it belonged to us."

"It belongs to international law. It belongs to all people."

"And we have an agreement with the government to cultivate the resources. That's one step away from colonization."

"That's completely different from colonization, C.C."

"I don't need you to say anything. I don't need you to agree to anything visibly. And I'm not taking command. But I need you to let Titan Space colonize. I need you to not argue when we plant our company flag."

"You know I can't do that."

"Do it for me, Em. I need a break here. I need this to go well."

"Too bad. You're not talking to me, you're talking to a government official."

"No, I'm talking to my friend, and I'm telling her to get out of the way of progress. Do this, and I can guarantee you the farthest-reaching mission in the galaxy. You can explore places nobody's ever dreamed of, Em."

"And now you're bribing a government official." She reached for her comm. He grabbed her wrist.

"Em, don't."

She glared at him until he removed his hand. Then she turned on the comm and said, "I'm heading back. Mission protocol and rank remains the same."

6

C.C. stood in front of a strange painting. If it could be called that. He wasn't an artist, and he didn't know his Picasso from his Dali. He knew art, as a concept, was good. It just wasn't for him.

"You're struggling with it. I can tell," said a voice behind him. C.C. looked over his shoulder. C.C. still had oil in his fingertips, but he'd at least been able to switch out shirts on the way to Jax Bennett's office.

"I'm sorry for my appearance, Mr. Bennett. We were changing out parts on the engine when I got your call."

Jax waved him off. "No problem. There's nothing better than getting dirty at work. It is a sign of forward momentum. I wish my hands were still covered in grease."

Jax Bennet wore casual blue jeans, suit jacket, and v-neck shirt combination that said he was easy going and not part of the old establishment, yet C.C. knew it was an outfit that probably cost more than most people make in two weeks.

Jax pointed to the painting. "It's a Roy Lichtenstein. It shows Cronos eating an apple, and Zeus plugging in a television set. I like to keep it out in the open where everyone can see it. Not because I expect them to 'get it,' but because they don't. You, like them, are an engineer. You see in requirements and rules and laws of physics. You have a hard time with art because there is no set rigor for defining it. How do you know something is art? You know it when you see it."

C.C. said, "I see a comic book panel."

"Exactly! Right there. You see form. You would give it function. Zeus is plugging in a television set. You would define the set: a Zenith. Ask an engineer to judge this painting, and he will have out a magnifying glass trying to determine what model of Zenith is being plugged in. But there is more than a television set. You have to ask why? Why is Zeus with the television and why is Cronos, his father, eating an apple?"

"Something about Adam and Eve and electricity?" C.C. didn't want to be here, but Jax Bennet was the CEO of Titan Space.

Jax clapped. C.C. wasn't sure if he was being insulted or not. Part of him wanted to punch the guy. But he hadn't joined Titan Space for the ordinary or for the usual. Jax Bennet was a Silicon Valley icon and a maverick entrepreneur who only broke into aerospace ten years ago. And that, C.C. was down with.

"That's it," Jax said. "Look, I know you see me as some wisecrack 20-something with more money than good sense."

C.C. protested perfunctorily, but Jax shook his head. "Let's be honest. I'm a guy who got a lucky break on computers. But then I got a lucky break on a renewable electricity technology. Then I got into a malaise. I thought I'd reached the pinnacle and would do nothing more. But that's when the government started talking about exo-planet exploration finally being viable. They wanted to partner, and I wanted the challenge. I saw myself as a kind of Elon Musk-meets-John Carter of Mars persona. And you know what? I liked me again. I started a company, made a few agreements, found some smart peeps like you to build these great Anchor ships."

Jax tugged C.C. away from the painting and over to the glass wall, which looked out over the long, wide warehouse that was the home of Titan Space. "See this? Over twenty-two-hundred individuals work here on engineering the Anchor. Worldwide, fifty-six hundred work for Titan Space. I'd do anything for this company. Like the great titans themselves, they are going to create the world as we will come to know it. You know in my first year, I had to sell my house in Malibu just to make sure my employees got paid? That's how important this is to me, C.C. You're probably wondering why you're here."

C.C. nodded.

Jax lifted a manila folder off of his glass table. He opened the folder and showed C.C. the file. C.C. knew the file well. It was his application to NASA to the astronaut selection committee. The file had a big "DNQ" (Did Not Qualify) stamped on it.

"The astronaut selection committee turned you down, C.C. They said there were some mild concerns about your ability to thrive in close quarters for a long period of time. But you know what? Expedition 18 is coming up, and I want you on it. So I talked to NASA. They are instating you. They are going to make you an astronaut."

Inside, C.C. was smiling. Externally, though, his demeanor didn't change.

"Come on, man. You should be happy. You're going to be all you can be. You had the right stuff. Well, most of it, at least."

"What's the catch?"

"The catch? No catch. You are going to be my guy. And that's going to come with lots of perks. Increased salary, your own parking spot, and of course the chance to visit an alien planet."

"All I have to do is represent you on this mission, though, huh?"

"No. Not me, C.C. You represent all of them." Jax pointed out of the glass window to the warehouse full of workers. "Their salaries are dependent on the continued success of our company. While you are away at 51 Golgotha a, your job is to remember that, and keep an eye out for company opportunities."

"Opportunities."

"What do you say?"

7

Downtime is always a problem for astronauts. Downtime leads to malaise, which is easy to succumb to in a tiny station or say, when your Ascent Vehicle has been destroyed and you have no chance of returning to the space vehicle orbiting your alien planet. Fortunately, the crew had a lot of tasks to complete while they waited a day for the solar cells to recharge the DSMU batteries. They would need them for their excursion into the desert to get to the monsters. They used the time to fix the Hab, which had sustained outer damage from the explosion.

During downtime, most astronauts have special areas of study and research that they explore. While Cole explored the Doomsday Book further, Anna conducted tests on a core sample she'd taken from the monsters.

First, she analyzed the sample for any biological material. She was in luck. She had some. Once she separated the biological material from the rest, she conducted several tests and worked to break down its DNA code.

She called everyone to come look because she had gotten so excited. "I think I've figured out how they got here."

"The monsters?" Cole asked.

"Mega Xenons," Anna corrected.

She pulled up several tests on her screen. They were all charts and graphs. "These creatures are amazing. The Mega Xenons have an incredible tolerance for radiation. It is a level of tolerance that we've never seen before. And their simplicity in design, the latticework structure of their cells means that the skin has a strength a thousand times stronger than human skin."

"Can you demonstrate?" C.C. asked.

She removed from a vial a purple piece of skin and placed it on the floor. The skin was about five centimeters thick. Anna looked around the Hab. She pointed to one of the only robots to not be destroyed in the crash. "OGRA, please."

The robot stepped forward and placed a foot on the skin. "It feels rubbery," OGRA said.

"How much do you weigh, OGRA?"

"This robot weighs 145 kilograms. Would you like me to convert that to pounds?" OGRA asked.

"We're good. Just step up onto the skin."

OGRA leaned forward, putting both feet and all of her weight on the skin. The skin did not show any sign of stress. It didn't sag in the middle or slip.

"Eish," Mathieu said.

91

"That's 320 pounds on a single layer of skin," Anna said.

"So it's strong, and it's very hardy against radiation. They are also tolerant to heat and cold. I tested the skin at over 300 degrees, and it was still living, and then I placed it with the LOX, and it survived that, too. I think what we are looking at is kind of similar to a water bear."

"Water bear?" Cole asked.

"A tardigrade," Anna said. "They are small, multi-cellular organisms long believed to be some of the hardiest creatures on Earth. The difference is they weigh less than a hairpin, and the Mega Xenons weigh as much as a mountain."

"So what does that tell us?" Emily asked. "They are tolerant of extreme heat and cold, they are incredibly strong, from a cellular standpoint, and they can withstand radiation."

"Don't forget, they have metal skeletons to help hold up the weight of their bodies," Mathieu added.

"They absorb energy wherever they stand, so they don't have to eat much," Anna added. "And they can enter hibernation for thousands of years."

"They're explorers, like us," C.C. said to Emily.

"Or colonizers?" Emily responded. "Do they land on a planet like 51 Golgotha and destroy all inhabitants so the planet is ripe for plunder when the rest of them arrive?"

Mathieu said, "The statue at the pyramid was pointing at the stars. Maybe it wasn't an extension of hope, but a reminder of what's to come."

"Monsters," C.C. said. "Sorry, Mega Xenons."

"Kaiju," Cole added. When the others sneered at him, he asked, "What? Am I the only one who likes Godzilla movies?"

"Well, we're going to have a chance to determine whether it is more monster or more kaiju when we go see it," Emily said. "Time's up. The DSMUs are ready."

8

The two-story-tall mechs struggled to traverse the desert topography. Except for the riddle of a second C.C.asaurus Rex skeleton that seemed to have been dragged under the dunes thousands of years ago, the crew encountered no new questions or adventures.

They pushed through the dunes, the sand sucking at the DCMUs' legs with every step. At this point, though, much of the lower half of the leg was just frame for spent boosters.

The trip took two hours longer than originally planned. Eventually they caught up with the giant monsters whose towering figures they'd been following all day.

"Crud," Mathieu said. "I think Cole's finally going to live his dream of meeting one of the aliens. The drones are showing that the Jedik-ikik are traveling faster than we thought. They're walking, though. Based on this data, we're projected to arrive before them."

"Do they look hostile?" C.C. asked.

"They have those blunt-edged spears with them."

"They're hostile. We should prepare for a fight."

"Don't be antithetic," Emily said. "They probably don't know we're coming. If we do meet them, we'll choose the peaceful path between our two peoples." She stopped and turned her DSMU on the others.

"Look, I know it's been difficult to say the very least, and the last two days have gone a lot worse than we ever expected. But that's no reason to give up on our training or our procedures. We were chosen for our ability to adapt, and we were trained to cope with loss. So dig deep into what you've learned. We're going to adapt and cope and whatever the hell else we need to do to get off this rock."

The monsters lay like mountains in the middle of the desert, their craggy peaks jutting out of the sand. The rock dragon and the three-legged monster, each fallen on their bellies, eyes closed.

"How do we know if they are alive or dead, or in stasis?" Cole asked. "I don't want to die if they get up and decide to stomp us into dust."

Anna held up her Health Sensor. "There is a heartbeat coming from over there." She pointed to the largest Rentok's foot.

"Its heart is in its foot?" Cole asked.

The DSMUs approached the mountains of monsters. The foot was the size of two rows of buses stacked on top of each other. Next to it, the DSMUs looked small. Maybe not like ants, but more like mice. Small, humanoid-shaped mice.

"If we direct the pulse cannon at the heart, maybe we can kill it," C.C. said. He didn't need to explain his maybe. Everything about these creatures defied scientific explanation. So while it seemed reasonable that destroying the heart of any other living creature would kill it, they really didn't know with these creatures.

C.C. climbed on top of the foot with Anna while the other three remained at the bottom. The pulse cannons charged.

And then a door opened in the base of the foot.

9

A thick, round astronaut's helmet appeared in the dark. Two blue eyes opened. Once the alien spilled out of the monster's foot, it became obvious that the eyes were circular blue goggles. The alien had a thick brow, nostril slits where his nose should be, two lower canines that jutted over his lip, and tapered ears. His skin was the color of old silver, the kind that stays in a bin and never sees daylight for years on end, and he had a blue pattern tattoo on the side of his face.

"What the?" Mathieu said.

The alien creature leaned against the rock and pushed his visor up. One side of the helmet was covered in blood streaks. The alien took several slow breaths. He looked unwell. He was weak, and possibly injured. He surveyed the astronauts while they exited their DSMUs.

"What do we say?" Anna asked. "Does he know Jedik?"

Cole stepped forward. For a moment, the alien and the astronaut watched each other, trying to feel each other out and see what the other would do. Then Cole took a big gulp of air and removed his helmet.He pointed to himself and said, "Astronaut." He pointed to every other crewmember and repeated the word.

The alien watched Cole pointing and speaking. His mouth moved like he was trying to speak. "TORnot," he finally said. Cole smiled. They were communicating.

But then something shorted in the thin electrical device the alien wore as a collar around his neck. He winced and pressed a button. "TORnot," he repeated. The device buzzed. "Stro-not," he said when he spoke again. And then the third time, "Astronaut."

"Yes," Cole said. "Astronaut."

"You are an astronaut," the alien said. As he spoke, little lights in the collar blinked.

"Yes. You can speak English?"

"No." He struggled for a minute, not just to find the words, but to find his breath. While the alien struggled, Cole placed the helmet back on his AXES suit and breathed in the oxygen. The rush felt good in his lungs. He wasn't so sure how much longer he could have gone on holding his breath.

"I am from the planet Gromm."

"How, how did you learn to speak?"

He pointed to his collar.

"But where did you pick up the English language?"

He pointed to the astronauts. "We have been listening to you since you arrived. We read your documents. You are here on a peaceful mission to study the Jedik-ikik."

"Yes."

"And you are here to colonize 51 Golgotha."

"Wait. No," Cole said.

"Yes," C.C. said.

The alien looked from Cole to C.C. and back. The alien's smile said a lot more about similar culture structures than Cole hoped to see in his lifetime. He just didn't know it at the time because he was trying to understand what C.C. was saying.

"We came from Gromm to colonize here, too. We came several times, but every time the Jedik repelled us. So we brought bigger and bigger Rentok."

"I'm sorry, but what are Rentok?" Cole asked.

The alien pointed to the monster behind him. "They call them Rentok. 'Destroyers of the Universe.' We call them vessels, though Rentok sounds much more interesting. We go as one, Rentok and pilot, to new worlds. For the worlds that can be harvested, we destroy the native civilization to prepare for colonists. The Jedik were too strong. They would destroy our vessels. When all was lost, we went into hibernation mode, knowing the Jedik would never reach us deep inside our vessels. We knew once the next group of Rentok arrived, they would wake us to join the battle. You woke us too soon. Now, without proper stasis rehabilitation equipment, I am dying."

The alien slumped to the ground, falling on his bottom and holding his stomach. Anna scanned him with her health sensor. "His heartbeat is weak, and he has internal damage."

"You," the alien said, pointing to Emily. "You finally beat me. You are Kroern Morrigan now. Come here. I have something for you."

"Don't do it," C.C. said, holding her by the hand, but Emily stepped forward. Cole approached with her. Together, they kneeled down on one knee next to the alien. He took off his glove. While the others watched in horror, hoping she would have the good sense to step away, Emily removed the glove from her AXES suit and took his hand. It was rough and aged, like an old book from a forgotten library.

"I pass on to you, Morder of Worlds."

"What'd you say?" Cole asked. "I'm sorry. Could you say that again? It didn't come through in your translator choker device."

"Nott," the alien said.

Emily felt a tingling in her fingers, and a bolt of electricity. She jerked her hand away. When she looked up, the alien was slumped back and looking up to the stars. He had stopped breathing. He was looking up to the stars. And the blue tattoo on the side of his face was gone.

"Baby," Cole said, disconcerted. "What's that on the side of your face?"

10

"I want to go inside," Emily said, her eyes to the door.

"Let's work the problem first," C.C. said.

"There's no problem here."

"We should analyze it."

"What is there to analyze? That the radiation out here is high? It's probably safer in there."

"I'm with her," Anna said.

The two women moved toward the door. Cole walked after them, then Mathieu, and then C.C. Mathieu stopped at the dead alien. He played with the translator for a moment, and then it popped off. "Hey, Cole, looks like you're about to become obsolete."

Cole looked up at the giant monster. "A lot of things are."

The room inside the Rentok's foot was dark except for three blue lights at the far end of the room. The astronauts turned on their helmet lights until Emily pressed one of the buttons and the lights came on.

"How did you know to do that?" C.C. asked.

She shrugged. "I've always had great analytical thinking." She pressed another button, and the outer door behind them shut.

"Too bad you don't use it," C.C. said. Emily scowled.

The small entry room had barely enough space for all the astronauts and their AXES suits. A set of spacesuits, like the one the Kroern pilot had worn, was strapped to one wall. Across from them was one door, with a spiral pattern on it. At the far end was another, but it had a slit down the middle. Next to the spiral door was another set of lights, and then also a small round door, not more than twenty centimeters in diameter, and about a meter off the ground.

Three tones beeped, each one lower than the previous. By the third tone, jets of gas were vented into the air.

"This is why we do the fault tree analysis, Em," C.C. said.

"We're okay. It's antimicrobial."

"This is an airlock." C.C. said what they were all thinking.

Once the venting stopped, Anna asked, "Which door do we take?"

Mathieu rapped the farthest door with his knuckles. "Metal. How do you get this much metal inside another living organism?"

Emily pressed another button, which was next to the nearest door. "Oops," she said, without any sense of apology. Inside, she was burning with curiosity. This was the kind of adventure she had wanted since she was a child first looking up at the moon and wondering what other planets were out there. It was the complete unknown, and she was drawn to it.

The flanges in the spiral door separated, revealing a second compartment even more cramped than the first. The flanges closed, and then a second door in front of the first. A series of buttons were on the side, as well as another circular door.

"Okay, so we are in an elevator inside a giant monster," C.C. said.

"Going up?" She pressed the top-most button. Without a sound, the elevator carriage began to move upward. Then it suddenly curved and turned upside down. The astronauts scrambled for the straps as they bumped over each other like leaves in a tossed salad. Just as suddenly, the elevator turned the other way and lay on its side. It shunted along like this until it turned them back on their heads, then quickly jolted the other way. The carriage came to a sudden stop.

The door opened.

"Get off my head," Mathieu said.

"Sorry," Cole said.

"No, not you. Your wife."

"Oh. Sorry."

Slowly the crew disentangled themselves from the mess they had become and left the elevator carriage. This was the biggest room so far, but it was still close quarters. There were six chairs around consoles. Each console showed a hologram of the giant monster's face.

"That is the face of one angry beastie," Mathieu said. He leaned in real close to the console to see the monster.

"You okay?" Anna asked him. In all the excitement, Mathieu had been able to get away with his vision problems. Not anymore.

"I'm fine. I've just been having a little vision trouble, but it's nothing that won't autocorrect itself," he said.

Anna pulled out a pen light and searched his eyes for trouble.

"You're not good," she said. "I need to get you to the Hab for observation."

"I'm as healthy as an ox."

"Maybe, but you're as healthy as an ox that's traveled through a seven year gauntlet of space radiation, only to fall to Golgotha. I need to do a more thorough review. I can't do it here."

"We'll head back soon," Emily said. "First, I want to get to know this beauty a little better. If I'm right, I can cut our travel time down to minutes."

The Rentok's face was covered in smooth rock patterns, like layers of sediment. Its teeth were like finely carved stalactites and stalagmites perfectly shaped over each other.

"He?" C.C. asked.

Emily nodded. "He is calling to me. I can hear him in my head. It is faint like he is yelling from a faraway window, and I don't understand his language, but he's calling for me."

She began to ascend the ladder at the far end of the room. It led to a higher platform.

"Where are you going?" Cole asked.

"I need to do something."

"Fault trees, Em," C.C. said. "Don't be a fool."

"Not everything is a fault tree, C.C. Sometimes you have to go with your gut."

They watched her ascend to the higher platform. Up here, the metals were mostly gone. Purple tissue surrounded most of the cabin. There was a console with another glaring face of the monster, and a chair. There were no circular doors on the walls, Emily noticed. There were several at the base of the chair, though.

She sat down in the chair. She was a little small for the seat, and the chair was cold.

From out of the flesh grew three purple masses, one from above and one from either side. The masses of flesh sought her out like feelers probing the air. As they approached her, the masses opened. Looking inside them was like looking at all the stars of the universe.

"Don't touch those things!" Cole called up to his wife. He was already climbing the ladder.

"I'm okay," she called back.

Tiny strands like thin tentacles reached for her. On a whim, she gave them her gloved hand. The mass reached around her glove, then jerked away.

"Why do I bother?" Cole grumbled.

She looked down at Cole and the rest of her crew. "Stop. I'm going to try something. Don't be afraid. Just…hold on a second."

Cole remained on his perch halfway up the ladder.

Emily removed her helmet and inhaled deeply.

"No, not that!" her husband cried out.

Anna checked her bio readings. "No, it's okay. We've been so excited we didn't notice that the readings are fine here. The air is breathable."

"How does it know what air we breathe?"

"It must have analyzed us when we first came in," Mathieu said while removing his helmet.

While C.C. and Anna removed their helmets, the tentacles twisted and turned, like the ends of a sea anemone waving in the ocean waters.

Emily twisted the cuff link to her glove and pulled it off. She held out her hand to the mass of tentacles while Cole cringed. The tentacles wrapped around her fingers, and then the mass extended over her hand.

11

Anger and pain rushed over her. A lonely, monstrous voice moaned in her head. She saw darkness, like living inside a giant sensory deprivation tank. After a moment, the moaning stopped, like something in the deprivation tank noticed her, and that notice made it stop its moaning long enough to try to understand the strange new creature in the tank.

"You are Renslot," appeared in letters in front of her.

While the moaning had stopped, Emily could still feel the rage and pain.

"I am Emily Musgrove, Commander…"

"Field Commander."

"Yes. My crew came to 51 Golgotha on an archaeological mission to seek out an alien civilization."

"And colonize," appeared in front of her.

"No! Well, maybe."

More letters. "I am a colonizer, too."

"Where are you from?"

A star chart appeared in front of her. A blinking green light showed 51 Golgotha. A blinking red light showed Renslot's home planet. It had a ring around it.

"That's far away."

There was a pause. Then the letters appeared. "The Kroern are space explorers and colonists."

"Your pilot told me." And as she spoke, she knew it to be true. The alien she met outside had been Renslot's pilot.

"Where am I? What am I seeing?"

"You are in my mind. This room is a representation of my mind, a construct to help bridge between pilot and Rentok."

"Why don't you talk to me?"

"I lack the vocal cords. I do not know what my voice would sound like. The pilots decided this would be a good way to communicate, though English is a much more cumbersome language."

"You are in pain. I can feel it. How can I help?"

"Just by being here, you are helping. But I need rest, and I need more of you."

"More of me?"

"More…contact…with you. My body was genetically engineered to deny me the ability to replicate and repair without a host. Without pilot contact. Your DNA will help fix my DNA. Your crew is hurting me."

"What? We are peace-seekers by nature."

"Then why are they stabbing at me?"

"They are probably scared for me. Return me to them, and I will find out."

"I have lost one pilot. I will not lose another. You are marked by Rezzik. That makes you mine."

Emily concentrated. She tried to return from the bridge. Renslot refused to let her go. She shook her head. "I must talk to my friends. I need to tell them what is happening and what the next steps are before I can help you. Please, Renslot. I want to help you, but I need to do this first."

The darkness pulled over her eyes, and she realized her eyes had never been closed. The darkness was the mass of tentacles rolling over her head.

As the light returned, she found herself surrounded by her crew. They had taken tools from their belts and were stabbing at the tentacles and the flesh.

"Are you okay, baby?" Cole asked, hugging her tightly. "We've got to get out of here. That thing was all over your head."

"Stop, baby. Everyone, I'm fine. I think it was supplying me with air. My eyes were open. Renslot got scared when you started attacking him. Funny to think of something so big frightened by what is, by comparison, so small."

"Who is Renslot?"

"All of this is Renslot. This, what'd you call it, baby? Kaiju? His name is Renslot. He's in pain, mostly because I shot him with our Ascent Vehicle. I wish I hadn't done that now."

"He would've killed us," Cole said.

Emily pursed her lips. She wanted to say something, but they wouldn't understand.

"To heal, Renslot needs more contact with my skin," she said. "It helps him to repair his damage, and since I'm the one who hurt him, I'm going to do it."

"More…skin?" Cole asked.

"Yes. I need everybody except my husband out of here."

"Now," she reiterated when they hadn't moved.

C.C., Mathieu, and Anna climbed down the ladder.

"I don't understand any of this," Cole said.

"I don't, either, and that makes me a little scared. We train to adapt, though, right? And part of adapting to the situation is making alliances to get us home. This has to be done." She kissed him. As she did, she could sense something from the Rentok. Was it jealousy? She couldn't be sure.

With the others downstairs, she climbed out of her AXES suit, then completely disrobed.

Cole said, "This feels weird."

"You're not the one standing completely naked inside an alien monster's body. Believe me, this is a weird that hasn't been invented yet."

"You should watch more anime."

She slapped him teasingly on the cheek. "Bad."

She sat back down in the chair and held her hands out to her sides.

"Wish me luck."

"How do I contact you?"

"I'm not real sure, but Renslot will keep an eye on you."

She could feel the warm tentacles move over the back of her hands, and then up her arms. A thought suddenly dawned on her. She tapped two circles on the floor. They slid open, and two more masses of purple flesh reached for her feet. As they wrapped around her extremities, she felt synapses exploding with connection.

Is this what it feels like to do drugs? She wondered.

Somehow the masses were breaching her skin and fusing with her nerves. They were exploring her whole nervous system from the inside out. She leaned back. The tentacles were up past her thighs. They were moving quickly up her chest.

"If you want this to stop, just say so," Cole said.

She shook her head.

From behind her, a giant mass appeared. It unrolled out of a compartment and wrapped around the back of her head like a soft blanket. As it moved over her eyes, the world went dark, and it stayed that way for a long time.

When she reopened her eyes, she learned that she was floating in a pool of black ink, with blue ripples that stretched out along a dark horizon.

"Relax" appeared above her head. The letters seemed made of fireflies. She reached for the word. The lights dissipated, the word disappeared.

Her arms were in her clothes. She was in her AXES Suit. The helmet was removed.

"Hello!" she called out. She waited for a response.

The fireflies returned. "Where did they come from?" she asked aloud as the little lights formed the word "Hello." Then, "Rest."

Emily *did* feel like resting. She leaned back in the pool of water. The water was warm, and so was her body. It wasn't like a bathroom where the air makes cold every inch of the bather's skin not submerged in water. She felt comfortable. At peace. And her suit was not wet. And neither was her skin or her hair. As soon as she rose up out of the water, it was like the water had never been there.

"How is this possible?"

"Rest."

She closed her eyes. She could feel the Rentok feeding off her DNA. She was sure it was purely symbolic, or most likely hyperbole, but in that moment she felt closer to the Rentok than she'd felt to anyone in her life.

She saw her mother. Not the body and shape of her mother the way she remembered her, but the way she remembered her mother from the womb. Everything was dark and pink, and she was an extension of her mother. Her mother's blood and nutrients were passing to her. She moved her fat little fingers and kicked in the womb.

"How is this happening?"

"You are unlocking memories you'd long forgotten. This is a byproduct of our bonding."

"I like the way this feels."

"You can stay here as long as you want while I repair us."

"I'm not damaged."

"So you say."

"Who are you?"

"They call me Renslot. To the Kroern I was TransGalactic Biological Entity First Assault Vehicle AG389."

"Certainly that isn't what your pilot called you."

Little lightning bug words did not form.

"Did I say something wrong?"

"I am trying to find a suitable word in your language. STD."

"STD?"

"I believe that is the acronym for…Sexually Transmitted Disease."

"Why did he call you that?"

"My kind are born with an STD. It prevents us from uncontrolled reproduction."

"That is horrible." She could hear pain in the creature's words, even if she could not hear them. Emily needed to change the subject.

"Tell me about the other Rentok I saw."

"There are at least three of us who survived. There may be more, but we have not been able to reconnect to them. One was captured by the Jedik. The Jedik call him the electric-eyed raven, K't'chimigalpa-kiritikikikee k'tang. The other has no Jedik name, but they call him Zree because he is so disruptive. Zree has always been temperamental, but now he is in more pain and anger than I."

"You don't seem angry."

"I am shielding my pilot from my anger because my emotions are transmittable. Besides, I am feeling better now. You are repairing me."

"Renslot, I want to feel your pain and anger."

"You are too new. Protocols protect you."

"Well, I'm the pilot, aren't I? So disable those protocols."

"My emotions are not worthy of a pilot's attention."

"Bullshit. And you know what else is bullshit? Your name. No creature should have STD for a name. I'm giving you a new one. How about Levia-gigantor-monstruoso?"

A smile appeared.

She shook it off. "I'm horrible with names. I'll have to ask Cole. Maybe he can come up with something better. In the meantime, stop stalling. Hit me with your best emotions."

Renslot did not respond. Within moments, though, she received what she'd been asking for. The rage was powerful and uncontrolled. Unmeasurable by human standards. Her body flexed in the seat as each wave of rage rippled over her.

She lost track of time in the rage. She lost all sense of the outside world. The anger was deep. It wasn't just anger at the events of its life, it was anger at being born. She pitied the state of the creature, and her pity angered it even more. So she stopped pitying the creature and yelled with it, deep inside its brain.

"Sandia," a voice said.

"What was that?" She kicked in the womb.

The words came again, stronger.

"Sandia Peak. South Trail."

Emily kicked again. "How much time has passed, Renslot?"

"Two hours."

"I need to wake up."

"Please don't."

"I will come back."

The mass moved over her face, and she was back in the cockpit, completely naked with her husband, who wore a mask of alarm on his face.

103

"What's happening? I heard you calling me." She pecked him on the lips. "Sandia Peak South Trail. That's perfect."

"The Jedik-ikik are approaching."

"Do you have the book?"

"Yes?"

"And the opening dialogue?"

"Memorized like my wedding day."

"Then we have everything we need. Let's go meet them."

CHAPTER 7: THOSE WHO TAKE

1

The rest of the crew were already in the access room at Renslot's foot. As Cole and Emily descended, this time strapped in so they weren't flung around pell-mell, Emily said, "Renslot is an amazing biological entity. Anna is going to flip out when she gets the chance to study him."

"He's an alien species."

"It's not just that, dear. He's a biomechanical entity. For instance, we're essentially traveling down a kind of an esophageal tract. We are moved up and down it by the tract. There is a sphincter above and below us. The Kroern must have surgically built a door in the tract that allows us to travel up and down the creature's body."

"Them. You mean it allows them to travel up and down the creature's body."

"Well, since we're the ones doing it, it becomes us, right?"

"Yes, but I don't like the way you say 'us.' You sound like you're including these monsters in the same group as your crew."

She reached for his hand. "Sorry, baby. Guess I'm getting carried away."

The door spiraled open.

"How far away are they?" Emily asked.

"They're already outside," C.C. said.

"That is less than ideal."

"They might think we are the Kroern. There is no guarantee that the Jedik-ikik and the Kroern have ever actually met except through these Rentok."

"That was our train of thought, too," Anna said.

"We need to communicate first that we are not Kroern but people from Earth, and then that we are here in peace," C.C. said.

Emily thought about it for a second. "First that we are not Kroern, but second that we are here to study and learn from the Jedik-ikik."

"Here to cooperate with the Jedik-ikik," Cole suggested.

"Good. Here to cooperate with the Jedik-ikik." She donned her helmet like everyone else, then said, "Renslot, please open the door."

Light flooded the access room as the door slid open.

Emily stepped out of the foot first, then waited for the others to stand at her side. Two hundred Jedik-ikik warriors surrounded the astronauts. They carried blunt spears and wore capes and jewelry, but nothing else.

A larger Jedik-ikik stepped forward. He was wider than the others, and his mandibles were like oddly-places bull's horns, they were so big. He studied the humans from behind his compound eyes.

Cole stepped forward. He said in the Jedik-ikik language, "Mighty Jedik-ikik, we are not the Kroern pilots of the Rentok behind us. My name is Cole-ikik. We are from the planet Earth, and we happened upon these creatures. We are here to explore this world and learn from its people, and to cooperate with its people."

The Jedik-ikik chittered their mandibles, especially the leader. He barked something at Cole angrily. "Krktlkknk."

Cole spoke slowly, saying, "Please slow down. I am still learning your language. We are having a hard time understanding."

"Trtz?" The leader said.

"Trtz," C.C. said. "Does he understand us?"

"The language is off somehow. There are fewer vowels than we thought. Give me some time with this. We weren't preparing for the aliens to come back to life and talk."

The Jedik-ikik pointed their blunt-edged spears at the astronauts.

"Slee! Slee!" Cole shouted. *Wait! Wait!*

"We don't have time for this," Mathieu said. "Here, try this." He bolted the translating collar around Emily's neck.

Emily repeated Cole's opening lines, though slightly modified: "Mighty Jedik-ikik, we are not the Kroern pilots of the Rentok behind us. My name is Emily-ikik. We are from the planet Earth, and we happened upon these creatures. We are here to explore this world and learn from its people, and to cooperate with its people."

The leader took a step back. "You understand us?" Because of the translator, she understood him perfectly. A quick glance to her fellow astronauts showed that they were not following the conversation as well as her.

"Yes," Emily said.

"I am formally known as T'tlit-klipfritchitipi-t'tltritz. I am a leader of these troops. How do we know you are not Kroern?"

"We come from over their mountains. Well, graves, I guess. We thought they were mountains, but they were really burial mounds. They tried to destroy our facilities, too."

T'tlit eyed the astronauts suspiciously. "You come from a far-star?"

"Yes. We come from a planet we call Earth."

"Only two types of people live here: conquerors and the conquered. Which are you?"

"Neither."

His mandibles twitched with frustration. The Jedik-ikik warrior didn't like this answer. In his world, it didn't make sense. He tried again.

"The land is conquered, the animals and plants are conquered. The zree Kroern are conquerors. Which are you?"

Cole, who was quickly picking up on the language changes, stepped forward and said the Jedik-ikik word for "friend."

The leader looked at Cole sharply. "You are conquerors from another planet. Seize them."

Several Jedik-ikik warriors had snuck up behind them while Emily talked to the leader. They knocked C.C. and Mathieu down. When Emily cried out, the mountain began to rumble.

"Cole, what'd you say?" C.C. snapped as he fell down.

"Conquerors! Friends of the invaders!" the leader shouted. They quickly cuffed the astronauts in stick-braces.

"Wait," Emily said. "You misunderstand us. We are not Kroern. The Kroern are all dead."

"All dead? How do you know?" T'tlit's second asked.

"He told us," Emily said, nodding to the dead Kroern pilot.

"The Kroern are liars. How do we know they did not send a message to more Kroern? I will tell you how. We do not know. And we do not know if you are friends of those zree Kroern."

"What if we can prove they are all dead?" Cole asked in Jedik-ikik.

"I would like to see that."

Cole turned to C.C. and said, "Show him the satellite photos, the ones showing the burial mounds with the metal skeletons."

"I would need my hands," C.C. said. Emily repeated this for the leader. The leader nodded, and C.C.'s cuffs were removed.

"He has a machine that shows pictures," Cole said in Jedik-ikik. "Those pictures will show the skeletons of the Kroern, and it will show that only the bones of their Rentok remain."

"They are called Rentok riders," T'tlit said. In his language, he used the phrase *Rentok Reitritz*.

Cole said. "Reitritz. I thought that meant another word in my language. *Raider*. It means people who sneak into a place and kill off the people there."

T'tlit sneered. "I think in my language, *rider* and *raider* means the same. Nobody rides who does not raid."

"Here," C.C. said. "Can you explain Emily or Cole? I think my language skills are a little below what's needed here."

The geo maps appeared as a 3D hologram of the mountains, with the metal skeletons inside. The Jedik-ikik warriors shouted when the image materialized. They had never seen 3D imaging before.

T'tlit reached for the image. When his hand moved through it, he reached back in shock. "How did you do that?"

"You come from a scientific society," Emily said, and the collar translated. "You can create automatons and projectiles and great structures. Maybe one day we will teach you how to create images like this. We used programs, similar to the ones you have in your automatons, but much more complicated."

The Jedik-ikik's mouth was an open rictus behind his mandibles. The nearest warriors cried out in dismay, as if a stage magician had just levitated the astronauts off the ground.

"This image shows geological structures, but it would also show living creatures under the mountain," Emily said. "Since there are no living creatures shown, the only conclusion is that all Kroern are dead, as the pilot over there said."

T'tlit walked away from the astronauts to confer with other Jedik-ikik. The crewmembers assumed this was a council of his highest-ranking officers.

While they waited, Cole tried to listen to the Jedik-ikik warriors, but his hearing wasn't good enough. He could make out that they were arguing about something, and he could guess what they were arguing about, but whether things were looking good or bad for the crew, he couldn't tell.

"I can't hear anything, can you?" he asked Emily.

"Yes." Since she still had the translator around her neck, and since Jedik-ikik guards stood nearby, she wouldn't say anything more. But when the leader and his council came back, she stood up straight like an officer about to hear her death sentence.

"You've made your decision?"

"We have decided you cannot be Rentok, but we do not know if you are Kroern yet. So we are taking you back to Ximortikrim to figure this out. We have several leaders there, and many scientists. They will help us understand who you are and what your goals are here on our planet."

2

The march was long and took almost the entire day to return to Ximortikrim. But their handcuffs were removed, and they were allowed to move around and talk as much as they pleased.

"I have a language question, leader of the warriors," Cole said to T'tlit.

"You can call me formally T'tlit-klipfritchitipi-t'tltritz."

"Thank you. That is my question, though. I work with linguists, people who study language. We have studied your language for years, trying to understand it. You say 'T'tlit-klipfritchitipi-tlirtz-ikik.'"

"T'tlit-klipfritchitipi-t'tltritz-ikik."

"Right. My apologies. That is a hard word for my mouth to make. But the final part, *ikik*, I thought it was a part of naming nomenclature. Like saying 'Mr. Musgrove.' But I think I am not quite right. I think it means more than Mister. That this is a formal name. An *ikik* name."

The leader thought about this, not slowing his stride. "Names are the most important words to my people. That is what *ikik* means. To not use *ikik* means that your name is worthless, and that you are worth nothing in the world. You are zeroed out. For example, the Rentok do not get the proper name. They are worthless to the Jedik-ikik. To give them that word gives them power they do not deserve. They are nothing more than a bunch of zree monsters."

"Can you tell us more about them?" Emily asked.

"I can, but I think it is more appropriate that better minded Jedik-ikik than me tell you. I am not a conqueror. I am the conquered."

The warriors shouted out, repeating what T'tlit said. *Trik Kilkree*. The Conquered.

3

The difference between Ximortikrim when they first entered it and Ximortikrim the second time they entered was as vast as the difference between a ghost town and an Olympic village at the height of the Olympics. Banners hung from freshly painted walls, streets were cleared of dust and debris, and fires were lit in the cauldrons. Automatons carried baskets full of fruit from the jungle.

On more than one occasion, as they were escorted through the streets, they happened to see Jedik-ikik dancing and singing to the crashing of cymbals and drums and very complex flutes that required all four hands to play.

From time to time, Jedik-ikik would stop and stare and point at the astronauts. At one point, an old Jedik-ikik approached them, screaming and spitting at C.C. One of the warriors removed the elder form the area.

C.C. said, "They think we are Kroern, don't they?"

"We will teach them the difference," Cole said.

"And when they don't believe us, what do we do then?"

"They will believe us. They have no reason not to."

"Part of being an astronaut is about planning for the worst things to happen."

"C.C. has a point," Emily muttered. "But now is not the time to discuss it. Just keep your eyes and ears open for possibilities."

Fortunately, the warriors were too taken aback by the revelry to hear Emily's words. The astronauts were delivered to the First Pyramid. There, T'tlit showed them to a room on the first floor, down the same hallway they had entered just two days ago. *Had that much changed in two days?* Emily wondered.

The room was sparsely decorated, but at the far end stood a table full of plant matter that the astronauts understood to be food. The room had been cleaned for them.

T'tlit said, "We are going to put you in this room. You will be taken care of. As a sign of trust, there are no guards, but please do not move from the room. I would not take pleasure from placing you in one of our only remaining holding cells at the Military Hall."

When they were alone, Emily removed the translator and pocketed it. "Thank you, Mathieu. That was a great idea."

"Sure thing, Emily. But what do we do now?"

Cole fingered some of the plants on the table. He looked at Anna. "Are any of these safe to eat?"

"That one will kill you slowly." She pushed through the plants, most of which were leaves and berries. "The rest of these will kill you quickly. See this one?" She picked up something that looked like a raspberry, but the size of a strawberry. "It contains a lethal dose of cyanide."

She picked up a limp sprig that looked like day-old grass. "Ah! This is Tweed Grass. You can eat all of it that you want."

"We are going to have so many Flight Rules when we get back to the Anchor," C.C. said. (Flight Rules were lessons learned for astronauts. Many years ago, they were provided after a mission, but on decades-long missions, they needed to be recorded as they were learned and documented in the Anchor's computers for return to Earth.)

"We can't fight our way out," Cole said.

"Speak for yourself," C.C. said. "Anna and Emily and I all served."

"I don't think we can take on the whole Jedik-ikik army, do you?"

C.C. did not respond.

Emily said, "Okay, but we know our way around here, and we've been studying this place for the past decade, so let's pull our information together and work the problem. I don't know when the Jedik-ikik are returning, but in the meantime, I want to plan out every option of escape we can find. I don't care if that means we're hang gliding off their pyramids. I want ways out of here."

The astronauts had less than two hours to make their plans. They did not have enough time to fully flesh out all their ideas, but the ones they did have, they made sure they were as lock-proof as an un-simulated plan could get.

T'tlit opened the wood-and-iron door. Five warriors stood with him.

In his language, he said, "Cole-ikik, you and your crew can come with us now. Thank you for not leaving here. Please follow me."

"Where are we going?"

"Not far. I am taking you to visit our Trik Kree-kikik."

They walked out. *Trik Kree-kikik.* The Supreme Conqueror.

4

Planets, moons, and stars moved along their mechanical orbits around the planetarium. Once again, the astronauts found themselves amazed at the technical abilities of this alien society.

Standing on a raised dais in the center of the room was Trik Kree-kikik. He had a bloated abdomen that weirdly reminded Cole of frogs. As they entered, T'tlit raised his arms above his head and placed his hands together, then bowed.

"These are the alien conquerors, Trik Kree-kikik," T'tlit said, motioning to the astronauts.

Cole mimicked T'tlit, bowing and forming an "A" with his hands over his head. "Hello, Trik Kree-kikik," he said in their alien language.

"I have many eyes, and yet I have never seen a creature that talks through a bubble," the Supreme Conqueror said.

"Pardon us, Trik Kree-kikik, but we need these suits to help us breathe here. Without them, your air would be poisonous to us."

"Do you have enough air to tell me your story?"

"Yes. These suits make your air clean for us. They don't store air."

"Good. But before you tell me your story, I must tell you about my people and about myself. We are a scientific people. We have not mastered technology the way your species has, but we know much about biology and medicine. I was ordained Trik Kree-kikik by the Scientific Council because my genetic code is cleaner and better than anyone else's. I am the best of my species. As long as I remain the best of my species, I will be Trik Kree-kikik. I will guide my people in scientific exploits, I will lead them in war, and I will breed a new generation of the Jedik-ikik."

C.C., like Anna and Mathieu, had a difficult time understanding most of the conversation. But C.C. picked up enough to say, "Interesting you should say that. Where we come from, people like us—astronauts— we're considered the best of the best. The cream of the crop." He said the last part slowly as the metaphor twisted his ability to translate it.

"The cream of the crop?" the Supreme Conqueror asked without understanding.

"The pick of the litter," Emily added.

Cole gave his wife a sideways glance. He didn't like where this was going. Idioms rarely translated well. At worst, they could be confusing and insulting. So Cole said, "What they mean is that astronauts undergo a rigorous selection and training process. Less than one percent of all astronaut candidates ever fly in space."

The Supreme Conqueror held his arms wide apart and stepped down off the dais. "You are genetically superior in your species? We must speak as equals, then!"

As he approached them, he said, "Of course, you must understand that you are not truly my equal, for you see, you may be the cream of the crop, but there are five of you. One of you is better than the others genetically. If we were to mate, our offspring would create the best of both worlds." He eyeballed C.C. as he said this.

"I don't think we would be compatible," C.C. said in his fledgling language skills.

"Besides, even if your offspring were to survive, they would likely be infertile," Anna added. She, too, was having a difficult time.

"I have an idea," Emily said. She removed the translator and handed it to the Supreme Commander. "Use this. We picked it up from the Kroern. It will change your words into our words, and for you, it will turn every word you hear into the language of the Jedik-ikik."

"Nothing the Kroern made will touch my skin."

Cole said, "We can spend the next three weeks stumbling through conversation, or you can wear this and we will all be able to understand you, and you will be able to understand us perfectly."

The Supreme Conqueror growled. "There is logic in your principles. I will wear this, but only for the duration of our conversation. Then I will return it to you. The Kroern are zree to us. To accept this could be seen as an insult to those who are not as smart as me."

The Supreme Conqueror put the collar around his head, and then he pointed to the star map. There was a star fixated far in the upper corner of the Planetarium. "This point here. This is the home of the Rentok Riders. They came here many thousands of years ago. They fell from the sky, nearly destroying our sister city Mirkitromix in less than a day. They nearly destroyed Ximortikrim, but we had our Izz." He held up the ceremonial blunt-edged spear. "Our engineers developed the Izz as a hunting weapon to kill giant Titititititilikikikiklit. We hunted them into extinction, and we tried to hunt the Rentok into extinction. We thought we did when we felled three of them, but when we dragged out their parasitic hosts, the Kroern, we learned to our disgust that the Kroern never give up on a world."

The Supreme Conqueror crossed the planetarium to the stairs. The astronauts and guards followed him to the wind tunnels overlooking the city. Cole remembered the room with the dead bodies. He wanted to ask the Supreme Conqueror about the bodies, but was recalcitrant to interrupt the leader. "So we looked for ways to defeat the Rentok Riders. We built this pyramid and erected the statues outside to remind us to always remain focused on the space-traveling invaders."

He pointed to the giant dome and to the aqueducts. "The Doomsday Engine was the first weapon. The Fire Path was the second. They helped us defeat the second and third invasions. Yesterday, some of those invaders rose up like the undead from their graves. Our Fire Path took down K't'chimigalpa-kiritikikikee k'tang, that zree Rentok. Like we did so many years ago, we were able to forcefully remove the parasite from the host."

The Supreme Conqueror pointed to one of the Fire Path aqueducts. A single body hung in a noose from the stonework high above the streets of Ximortikrim. The alien, which looked similar to Renslot's pilot, wore a pair of blacked-over goggles.

"This is what we do to invaders," the Supreme Conqueror hissed.

"We are not invaders."

"We will find out soon." His tone had shifted. He seemed to stand over them now, a hunched statue of a wasp wielding a giant scythe.

"T'tlit-klipfritchitipi-t'tltritz-ikik, my warrior who found you, approves of you. He is a good conquered, but he is no conqueror. I will decide if you are here as a blessing from science or as something far more sinister. Where is your spaceship?"

Emily said, "Supreme Conqueror, you will find that we come in peace. Our spaceship is in orbit above your planet."

The Supreme Conqueror snapped his fingers, and a strange telescope was presented.

"Prove it."

C.C. tried to make eye contact with Emily, but she was too far away. He wanted to warn her, but there was no need.

"Regrettably, I cannot do that. My orders are to never tell the location of the spaceship."

"That is wise. But is it important enough a secret to trade death to your conquereds?"

"Don't tell him," Mathieu said.

"Ditto," Cole added.

"If you are truly on a mission of peace and scientific discovery, prove it. Show me your space ship."

"You must trust me."

"The last aliens we trusted destroyed Mirkitromix, and nearly destroyed Ximortikrim. *If you need, you will be provided. If you take, then home will be as unknown to you as the mind of the Rentok.*"

The threat was obvious. Emily was cool in the face of it, though internally she was trying to figure a way around this. She didn't know why she hesitated to reveal the Anchor. The Jedik-ikik lacked the ability to fly into low Golgotha orbit. Their research would have uncovered that capability. So why was she hesitating?

And what is that ringing in my ears? She'd never experienced tension headaches before. She was feeling one now.

"We are not takers," Emily said. "We are needers." She checked her watch and pointed to the Northern hemisphere. "You can see it. You don't need a telescope. The small blinking light in the sky? That is the Anchor."

"Amazing," the Supreme Conqueror said. "You are truly a people of the impossible to have learned to fly into space. We have only been able to send things in space, not retrieve them. For example," he gave an order to a guard who was holding a small mechanical flying machine. The guard wound up the flying machine and tossed it in the air. The machine sprouted wings and glided out of the wind tunnel toward the Doomsday Engine.

"What are you doing?" Emily asked crossly.

"Be calm," the Supreme Conqueror said. The Jedik-ikik around them raised their blunt-edged spears, their Izz.

"Watch." He pointed his ceremonial spear to the center of the city. The winged machine fluttered, then descended into the open space where the dome was broken. Moments later, the dome began rotating.

"Don't do it," Mathieu said, the reality of the situation dawning on him. "You will cut off all ties we have with our home world, hey."

Trik Kree-kikik held out two of his hands for the astronauts to examine. "Notice how steady my hands are? I point this out to you so that you know I am not angry or emotional. I have a genetic predisposition to even-tempered judgement. I want you to know this because I want you to know that I did not sentence you to spending the rest of your lives on my planet out of anger, but because it was the most sound logic to protect my Jedik-ikik."

But the astronauts were not looking at his arms. They watched the bright light bursting out of the dome and streaking up into the sky. Cole held out hope that the Jedik-ikik had missed their spacecraft. The Anchor was listening to their every conversation. Perhaps it adjusted its flight pattern once the Supreme Conqueror described his plan?

"We knew from our first encounters that the Kroern would come at us from the sky, so our engineers developed the Doomsday Engine to remove that threat. The Doomsday Engine was the cause of death of most of the Rentok that came after the first invasion. But we knew we would need a way to fight them from the ground. We built a network of aqueducts that could channel both magma and water. The result is the K't'chimigalpa-kiritikikikee k'tang sitting out there."

He pointed back to the aqueduct. Cole thought that between the Doomsday Engine, the aqueducts, and the fallen Rentok, he was seeing a tryptic of doom. Or maybe the conquered and the conqueror? The cataclysmic view was capped off by the streaking pieces of the Anchor falling through the atmosphere in a fiery wave.

"You monster!" Cole shouted. "You dumb, stupid monster. Do you realize what you've done?"

The Supreme Conqueror pointed his Izz spear at Cole's face. "I see not all of you are scientific minded. A pity."

"A pity?" Cole shot back. "And were you so callous when Mirkitromix was destroyed?" Cole began cussing in different languages.

"Cole, shut up," Anna grunted through her tears. "You're going to get yourself killed."

Already, the Supreme Conquerors guards were approaching Cole.

"He's okay," Emily said.

"You should remove him from your equation before he kills you all," Trik Kree-kikik said flatly.

"I need him for my own multiplication."

The Supreme Conqueror stood there and digested Emily's equation for a moment. Then he said, "I do not agree with your formula or your tactics. Perhaps in the years to come, I can help you to better understand how to best propagate your genetic code."

"How did you do it," C.C. asked. "How did you hibernate for thousands of years?"

Trik Kree-kikik welcomed the change of topics. He held out a vial for them to see. "This was to be our salvation. Should the creatures not be destroyed while still in the sky, and should they prove more powerful than our network of channels, then the final prevention would be the Sleep Key. It is buried in the ground, as you have probably ascertained, underneath the statue of its inventor, the great Kittrik-ikik, who was killed in a horrible accident when he discovered the Sleep Key. The Sleep Key is a biological entity, a parasite that causes whoever it touches to fall asleep forever. It creates a stasis that keeps the host alive while it reproduces and moves along to find other creatures to touch."

"Why didn't it affect us, then?" Emily asked.

"The parasite can only live for up to three days in our atmosphere, approximately 108 hours. By our analysis, we have been asleep for over four thousand years."

"That is our analysis, too," Emily said, but she was thinking of the family locked away in the hidden chamber, with 93 notches carved into the wall. They had almost outlived the Sleep Key.

"We woke you, somehow," Anna said.

"After the parasite has finished its life cycle, then in the presence of a second biological entity, such as yourself, the effects of the Sleep Key dissipate. If everything else failed, I was to give the retreat order. Everyone would return to bunkers high up in the pyramids, where they would be safe from the Sleep Key because it cannot climb more than 30 meters. The Sleep Key would silence the Rentok, but the Sleep Key would be prevented from affecting the rest of our planet by our high outer walls. See, you thought those walls were erected to keep things out. They were really to keep things in. After the Kroern were asleep, our robots would exorcise them of their demon parasites, and their homeworld would be none the wiser.

"Unfortunately, a warring faction released the Sleep Key before I could issue the command to retreat. They saw the Key as an opportunity for genetic purification, that it would put everyone and the Rentok asleep, and then they would cull the weak from our population while they were sleeping. They announced this as they turned on the Sleep Key. It was a horrible day for the Jedik-ikik. To finally have a solution to the colonizing Kroern, only to have a small group of our own use our weapon against us."

For a moment, the Supreme Conqueror stared out at his city. Jedik-ikik do not cry. They lack tear ducts. But Cole noticed that when they were emotional, their mandibles chittered constantly. The Supreme Commander tried to hide it, but his mandibles opened and closed in a quick spurt like a small sob from a child or the single tear of a soldier.

"Thankfully, they were not able to survive the Sleep Key and fell into a catatonic state like the rest of us. When your presence woke our city, the first thing we did was purge Ximortikrim of this warring faction."

Emily thought of the first drone images of the city after they discovered the Rentok. Jedik-ikik were executed. It had seemed strange then, but made sense now what she was seeing.

A small ripple of a Golgothaquake vibrated in the room. Guards rushed in.

"It seems the Kroern are not yet dead," the Supreme Conqueror said. He removed the communicator and handed it to one of his guards. He said, "Take them to the network, with the other pilot. Hand them over to the Old Devil, and tell him I don't want them back until he has all the information about the Kroern. Give him this so that he may be able to understand their words."

"But we are not Kroern," Emily said in the Jedik-ikik language.

"Are you saying that the greatest mind in Ximortikrim is wrong?" He stood with his arms akimbo and dared any of them to tell him otherwise.

When they did not respond, he ordered the crew taken away. "We have preparations to make. The Rentok will not survive this time."

5

Twenty Jedik-ikik troops escorted their prisoners out of the First Pyramid and across the battlefield to the network of aqueducts. To get there, the escort circled around the giant tower that had become the Rentok, K'tang. From the bottom up, K'tang was like standing at the base of the Statue of Liberty and looking straight up. Unlike the Statue, though, K'tang was covered in molten lava, which left eerie black patterns in the giant shape, which had arms stretched out to the aqueduct channels.

The troops stopped at the far end of K'tang. One of their escorts, the one with the collar, entered a tent that had been erected there. While they waited, Emily surveyed the area for anything that could help her. She noticed that the door was open at the end of K'tang's foot.

From the tent emerged the Old Devil, wearing the translator. He was a tall, hunched Jedik-ikik with long scars stretching up and down his torso. One of the eyes on his long face was caved in. When he spoke, his voice was hard as iron and sharp as a circular saw.

"Captain, your men are dismissed. Leave these wretched aliens to me."

As the escort left, the Old Devil watched the astronauts scornfully, like a rancher trying to decide which cow-killing coyote to shoot first.

He was a resolute Jedik-ikik, stern in his hatred. As the ground trembled, he stood tall. When he spoke, he spoke matter-of-factly.

"If it were up to me, I'd kill you zree now and not think twice of it. But my Supreme Conqueror wants you to stay alive long enough to give up your secrets."

He nodded to Mathieu. The Old Devil's troops pulled him in front of the others.

"You look like the strongest of your group. Your helmet. Why do you wear it?"

"I cannot breathe your air."

"The Supreme Conqueror does not want you dead quickly, but I don't care about these things. If you die, there are four others. Remove your helmet, or I will smash it."

Mathieu looked to the other astronauts. Emily wished she could break through the pain in her head. She said, "Do as you're told, Mathieu."

Mathieu took several quick breaths—inhale, inhale, inhale—and pulled off his helmet. The soldiers took his helmet and placed it on a table.

The Old Devil smiled fiendishly. He motioned for a bucket to be brought to him. Two soldiers brought forward a heavy, black bucket. They carried it on two long poles, and placed it on a wooden stoop that groaned with the weight of the bucket. The bucket had a lid, and a set of tongs hanging from opposite sides.

"The goal of torture is to receive information from you that you'd rather hide. Most of my soldiers think the best way to do this is to cause you significant pain. If the pain is bad enough, you will talk. But they are wrong. Research has proven that the best way to get your secrets is to give you something in return. The absence of pain, for instance."

He stopped and said to Mathieu, "Still holding your breath? Keep holding."

Emily thought of their breathing trials. Mathieu could hold his breath for almost a minute and a half. That was supposed to be good knowledge in case a suit was compromised. This was another thing entirely.

"I need something I can give you in return," the Old Devil clucked. "But what?" He strummed his fingers on Mathieu's helmet while smiling.

He stopped and studied the expressions on the astronauts' faces.

"We come in peace," Emily said. "We mean you no harm."

"You must be their leader."

"No, I am," Cole said.

The Old Devil laughed. "Don't play me. You're clearly the most conquered in this group." He looked back at Emily. "What is your name?"

"Commander Emily Jane Musgrove."

The Old Devil smiled. "Give him his helmet back."

The soldiers handed Mathieu his helmet. He put it over his head just as he was starting to go blue in the face. He vented the atmosphere and gasped in the oxygen.

"See how well this works? You give me information, I give you air. The absence of pain is the information channel, not the pain itself. Now, the first thing you do when torturing a group of people is you show them how much power you have over them. They need to believe in that power. It is an important step. The way you prove your command is by utterly defeating their strongest member. Take his helmet back off."

"No!" Anna shouted, reaching for Mathieu. One of the troops stood in her way.

Mathieu took several quick breaths.

Inhale. Inhale. Inhale.

The soldiers pulled the helmet off of him.

The Old Devil looked up at the behemoth towering over them. He breathed in deeply.

"Twenty under my command are buried in the lava flow beneath this monstrosity. Did you pilot the zree Rentok, K't'chimigalpa-kiritikikikee k'tang?"

"No," she said.

The Old Devil motioned, and the helmet was placed back over Mathieu. He gasped immediately.

"That was an easy question. Even I knew the answer to that. The pilot's hanging up there." The astronauts followed where he was pointing to the body, swaying in the wind.

"Now, some harder questions. Remove his helmet."

Inhale. Inhale. Inh—

The helmet was ripped off him.

"Are you Kroern?"

"No."

The Old Devil's only eye traced down at her.

"Are you Kroern?" he demanded, more resolutely.

Already, Mathieu was turning blue in the face.

"We are astronauts from planet Earth. We are here to study and learn from your people."

"What is 'astronaut?' The word does not translate."

"It means we travel through space to learn about the galaxy."

"Space?"

"Astro means space," Cole intervened. "Naut means person who journeys. The roots of these words come from an ancient language from our world."

The Old Devil turned his gaze to Cole and calculated his next question while Mathieu gave out and started sucking in unfiltered atmosphere.

"Space journeyers?"

"Yes," Emily said. "Like your people, we believe in science and education. We are here to learn from you, but we thought everyone was dead. We didn't know anything about the Kroern, we didn't even know the mountains were Rentok. We didn't even know what the word 'Rentok' meant."

He leaned down close to her helmet. "Now that is good conquered truth."

The helmet was placed back on Mathieu. The soldiers cuffed his hands behind his back. Mathieu coughed and gasped in the dirt, but he did not get back up.

"Can I tell you the good conquered truth I know?" the Old Devil asked.

"Sure." Emily said it in a way that couldn't care less. She reached for Mathieu with her eyes, but she couldn't see his face.

"That was difficult to give up, I know. You had to admit that everything you've done has been a mistake. I want to reward that. But before I give you my conquered truth, I must tell you the second part of torture. We have a relationship established, you and I, Commander Emily Jane Musgrove. But you will always trip it up. So my goal is to find your lie and exploit it." He growled knowingly, but Emily had no idea where he was going with this.

He continued, saying, "I spoke to the Kroern hanging up there, and he told me that there were many Kroern, and that they would not stop coming until our world was colonized and the Jedik-ikik were either enslaved or wiped out. I asked him how could a little zree like him pilot such a large monster. He told me his mind was melded with the monsters. He told me I would always know the Rentok Reitritz by this." The Old Devil brushed his hand against the tattoo on Emily's face.

Emily pulled away from him. "I did not know what I was receiving."

The Old Devil nodded with understanding. He returned to the big black pot. With one hand, he pulled from underneath his cape what looked to be a set of deep cups, or goggles. He put on gloves and nodded to Mathieu.

"No, please don't," Emily pleaded.

"Don't worry. I will put his helmet back on soon."

Carefully, the old Jedik-ikik warrior pulled the caps half-way off of the goggles. Then he slid the lid off of the heavy bucket ever so slightly. It left an opening big enough for his tongs, which he then used to poke around in the pot, like he was picking a good fruit. But instead of a fruit, he pulled out a small, wormy insect like a centipede. It had two longer front legs, each with a giant hooked pincer. The small creature was like a cross between a centipede and a scorpion, but covered in spikes. It writhed in the eyepiece.

The Old Devil glanced at the astronauts, who watched in horror as he plucked another tiny nightmare and placed it in the other goggle.

"What is that?" Anna asked. "I thought there were no creatures but you remaining on 51 Golgotha."

"The Sleep Key escaped over our broken walls and infected the forest, killing most creatures there. Fortunately for these creatures, they thrived in the desert wasteland, and the Sleep Key did not invade that far."

A giant roar ricocheted off the pyramids. Everyone turned, even the Old Devil. The Rentok were not in sight yet.

"We must hurry this up," he said to Emily. He closed the bucket and the goggles, then he strapped them to Mathieu's face. Mathieu was so tired and confused, he barely struggled against his captors.

"This creature feeds on the fleshy innards of a juicy nut that falls from a rare desert tree. It will do anything to get inside those nuts, even chew through stone and wood and of course, the thick wall of the seed. We learned that we can use that voraciousness to our own means. You are going to tell me everything about the Kroern."

"I will tell you everything you want to know," Emily bawled. "Just don't hurt him anymore."

He placed his claws on the goggle's caps. "You are forgetting the rules, Emily. First I pick the strong one out of the group."

"No!"

"And then I destroy him."

"Don't open those goggles! You don't have to do this. I will tell you everything, I swear. We are on a mission of peace."

"I have no way to know for sure until after I have destroyed your strongest. That is the formula. Then you will tell me what I want to know, or I will do to the rest of your friends what I am going to do to him."

The Old Devil pulled back on the caps. The little worms squirmed in the lenses. Though he'd been half-way unconscious from oxygen deprivation, Mathieu jolted awake, screaming.

6

"No more!" Emily yelled, straining against her wooden handcuffs.

"Restrain her," the Old Devil said. Two of his soldiers approached her with additional bracers, when suddenly she reached out and popped one on the chin so hard Muhammad Ali would be proud. A fierce sound came out of her chest as she jumped at the second soldier approaching her.

Behind the city, a second roar of untethered anger bellowed out. The Old Devil looked over his soldier. The mountain peaks were back. They were silhouetted against the sky, rising over Ximortikrim's outer wall. The Destroyer of Worlds had arrived.

The Old Devil shouted his order to attack.

Emily seized the opportunity to steal one of their spears and embrace its implementation against an unsuspecting soldier. The soldier's insides exploded.

She was now close enough to Mathieu. She ripped off his helmet and then his goggles. Two deep gouges looked back at her. She could see the worms burrowing in his orbits. She grabbed the tongs and pulled the first one out. The little creature zigzagged its body in her tongs. She flung it toward the soldiers.

Mathieu groaned as she probed his eye socket for the second worm. *Good*, she thought. *I know you're alive.*

She pulled it out and flung it just as soldiers grabbed her.

The Old Devil said, "There may be a link between her and Renslot. Hang them all. Now. The quicker, the better."

7

A surly group of soldiers took the astronauts to the aqueducts while Renslot slammed into the city wall. A mass of rubble and troops went flying. The rock dragon looked around as if searching for something. Below him, Jedik-ikik warriors jumped onto his feet and began the long climb up his mighty legs. It was like climbing a tornado. As Renslot moved, north became west, and wind rushed around the soldiers. But they knew Ximortikrim's survival depended on their courage, so they clung to Renslot's crags in the hope of being able to bring him down.

Renslot pushed into the city, running toward a pyramid. His body bashed into the ancient pyramid, leveling it. All the while, more and more Jedik-ikik warriors climbed his legs and waited for the pheromone signal.

Behind Renslot, another beast's onerous war cry thundered across the sky. The three-legged Rentok had returned for his vengeance. The giant monster limped toward the Doomsday Engine at the heart of the city. The Doomsday Engine slowly cranked around to face the giant monster. While the ungainly giant gained speed, he crashed through the city buildings like a rhinoceros running wild through African huts. Stores and offices were crushed under his feet, and their remains scattered from his footfall. While all this destruction was going on outside, inside the dome, engineers loaded the weapon and began fueling. Just as the fueling completed, the giant monster rammed into the great dome. And just as Renslot had learned, the beast realized that the dome was too well built to be crushed or smashed.

Down below, like bees in a hive, the Jedik-ikik engineers felt the crushing blows of the zree on the dome. While they knew the dome was powerful enough to survive the first attack, they didn't know if it would stand up against a second. They had not fully repaired the dome since the greatest of apocalypses, the Renslot, attacked them, digging at the dome's infrastructure.

Soldiers were sent to try to gain the engineers some time. Firing the Doomsday Engine was not as simple as turning a key or pressing a button. There were protocols to follow to ensure that the rocket did not explode and take everyone in the dome with it.

Outside, the giant monster tried wrenching the barrel back and forth, but it was too well-constructed for that attack. The barrel was one full meter of thick iron all around.

Jedik-ikik warriors climbed onto the monster's feet. They were the first to get there. Down the central street, they saw a patrol running down the street toward them.

8

Two Jedik-ikik climbed on top of the aqueduct. From far away it had seemed small, but on the ground and up close, it had at least a three-meter tall lip on top of a half-meter embankment. Two warriors climbed to the top of the lip. One went over and into the aqueduct. While the warriors lifted each astronaut up, the Jedik-ikik on top of the aqueduct lip grabbed them by their shoulders and lifted them over the wall.

Once inside the aqueduct, very little of the battle could be seen from within its steep walls. One of Renslot's peaks came into view, and then they heard the monster venting his anger on Ximortikrim. Something exploded, and dirt and rubble were flung over them.

The Jedik-ikik pushed the astronauts forward. The aqueduct rose up in the sky before them like a roller coaster from Hell.

As they were marched up the aqueducts, Renslot continued his angry advance on the city. He found a hidden armory full of explosives, which blew up in his stony face. He stumbled backwards and then doubled down on his anger, plunging his monstrous face into the pyramid. It was full of Jedik-ikik. He opened his mouth, and a wave of cosmic radiation shot from his mouth. The light from the blast echoed out of the buildings windows and doors. He sniffed the building like a bear looking for honey. Unsatisfied with what he found, he dropped to all fours off of the building and moved on to the next colossal pyramid.

By then, almost fifty warriors were on his legs and feet.

At the center of the city, the warriors began their climb up on the giant monster. They'd taken one leg. They could take the other three. At least that's what they shouted to each other.

As for the giant monster, he continued trying to destroy the Doomsday Engine. He tried reaching for the engineers. He was more effective in this than Renslot had been. One of his arms ended in a sharp mountain face, which he used like a shovel to dig into the dome's innards.

The ignition sequence began.

In the bowels of the dome, a thick door opened, and an engineer wearing aluminized shielding entered the enclosed chamber. Above him loomed the rocket's nozzle. Below him were caverns with a thin red line of magma very far below. Nervously, he walked out onto the stone support landing and approached the nozzle.

"Klilbit," another engineer announced over a speaker system. Fumes spewed into the room. The engineer lit the stick in his hand. Showers of sparks shot from the stick like a Roman candle. He heard a poof, and then a THOOM as the fumes ignited. The blast knocked him back off of the landing next to the door. Already he could feel the intense heat burning out of the engines. Smoke plumed outward. Out of the smoke, two more engineers in heat shielding appeared, dragging him back through the open door and shutting it.

Clouds of exhaust burst out of the dome and all around the three-legged monstrosity. At the same time, the Jedik-ikik gave their pheromone command. Concussive blasts swarmed over the monster's legs.

The creature shouted its fury, then spewed its fury all over its legs. Magma boiled and bubbled over his legs, melting the soldiers in their hiding spots. Unlike frozen K'tang, this one was accustomed to magma and easily stepped out.

Then a thought came to him. He smiled down on the engineers. He put his mouth over the cannon's giant barrel and vomited magma into the core. Over and over he vomited until the magma was dripping out of the sides. Then he walked away from the dome.

The engineers knew there was no stopping the sequence. They tried to run from the dome, but did not make it to the door before the entire dome exploded.

A giant fireball shot into the sky.

A concussive blast rocked through the city, toppling statues and columns and doing more damage than the Rentok had ever done.

The blast was enough to knock the magma-belching monster to the ground, which created a giant aftershock that blew over the ancient city, knocking out windows and intricately tiled murals.

9

Exhausted, legs burning from the uphill hike, the astronauts arrived at the top of the Fire Path. Now they could see K'tang entombed in magma below them. A thick rope lay tethered to the end of the channel. They didn't want to think about what was on the other end of the rope.

Three warriors hammered spikes into the channel's floor while the other five held on to the astronauts. Only Mathieu was not standing. Back at the Old Devil's camp, when these soldiers were ordered to hang them, the soldiers did not put Mathieu's helmet back on his suit, so he had been breathing in carbon monoxide ever since. When they dropped him on the floor of the channel, his body fell limply. Emily wondered if there was any life left in him because some part of her still felt they could escape this. They were astronauts, weren't they? They had trained to deal with any problem and improvise with whatever other calamity fell in their direction. And yet, another side knew that if he was already dead, his suffering would be over.

The soldiers started bashing in the helmet visors one-by-one and tying knots around the necks of the astronauts.

C.C., who had been quiet this whole time, shoved his shoulder into the body of the Jedik-ikik coming at him with a rope. The Jedik-ikik fell backward, and C.C. kicked him off of the channel.

A second soldier kicked C.C. off of the channel, and the rope snapped tight around his neck.

Suddenly, the dome exploded, and the fireball scorched the sky.

"Hurry," one of the soldiers said to the others. "We must return to battle."

Anna was dropped over the channel next. The soldiers moved Cole and Emily, who were trying to brace their feet against the floor to keep from being thrown over.

"That's my wife," Cole growled in Jedik-ikik. "Don't any of you have wives?"

Then the love of his life was gone over the side of the channel.

The soldiers grabbed Mathieu.

"I have something you want," Cole said. "The Doomsday Book. I will give it back to you, but first you have to pull my friends back up." The words were coming easily to him now.

"We will find it, eventually. If not, we can rethink it."

"Of course, because you are a scientific people. But you are also a people of words. I know words are important. I see them etched into your walls and sewn into your banners. Special words. Specific words." He coughed. His head was starting to hurt.

"Words are only useful for transmitting information," the soldier said.

"Information about science and technology. Yes. But also feelings and emotions. Thoughts and ideas. I want to recite you something from my people. Something that explains us, and if you still think we are here out of some unseen malice, then you can throw me over and I won't fight you."

The soldier moved toward Cole.

"We choose to go into space."

The soldier stopped. Cole coughed.

"We set sail on this new sea because there is new knowledge to be gained, and new rights to be won, and they must be won and used for the progress of all people. For space science, like all science and all technology, has no conscience of its own."

The soldiers stood back.

Cole continued. He knew the words. Of course he knew them. Who in the astronaut corps hadn't heard the speech at least a dozen times? The words came easily to his mind, if not from his lungs, which felt like syrup. "Whether it will become a force for good or ill depends on us, and only if...we help decide whether this new ocean will be a sea of peace or a new terrifying theater of war. I do not say that we should or will go unprotected against the hostile misuse of space any more than we go unprotected against the hostile use of land or sea, but I do say that space can be explored and mastered without feeding the fires of war, without repeating the mistakes that man has made in extending his arms around this globe of ours.

"There is no strife, no prejudice, no national conflict in outer space. Its hazards are hostile to us all. Its...exploration...deserves the best of all mankind, and its opportunity for peaceful cooperation may never come again. But why, some say, the Moon? Why choose this as our goal? And they may well ask, why climb the highest mountain? Why, thirty-five years ago, fly over the oceans?

"We choose to go to the Moon...Not because it is easy, but because it is hard; because..."

Cole stopped. He looked up at the sky behind the Jedik-ikik and coughed. They followed his gaze. Two giant, stone faces grimaced down at the soldiers.

The soldiers dropped their weapons and ran back down the aqueduct. The Rentok watched them go. Cole strained against the ropes to pull his friends and family back up. First, his wife. He wasn't even sure she'd survived the fall, or if her neck was snapped. Fuck it. He refused to acknowledge the second thought. Hand over hand, her body rose back up. She squirmed in the rope as he pulled her over the ledge. He pulled the rope from around her neck, and she gasped for air. The unclean air might as well have been toxin in their lungs.

They kissed quickly and pulled Anna up. Then a giant hand appeared and carefully scooped the astronauts up out of the air and placed them back in the channel. Renslot growled pleadingly at Emily.

Ropes were pulled off.

Cole was seeing stars. His wife shook her head from some unseen pain. They needed to act fast or die. Wilderness expeditions in the Rocky Mountain wilderness of Montana had prepared them for working together on life or death experiences. So had multiple failures onboard the Anchor during their trek across the galaxy to 51 Golgotha.

They each grabbed a piece of Mathieu's AXES suit and began jogging down the channel to the giants' feet. They didn't pay attention to all the destruction on the horizon: the trails of smoke from fires, the smashed pyramids, the dead bodies lying in the streets of the dead city. They concentrated on getting to the door.

They just had to get to the door.

Inhale.

Cough.

Inhale.

Cough.

"Mellifluous," Cole said.

Anna coughed. "Mellifluous," she said.

"Calm," Cole said.

"Calm," the whole team repeated.

"Balanced."

"Balanced."

"Serene."

"Serene." Emily stumbled.

"Mathieu, C.C., and Anna can go fuck themselves."

Emily laughed first. Then the others laughed. They were almost half-way down the aqueduct. Renslot gently placed his foot on top of the lower aqueduct. The stone splintered and cracked, then obliterated into dust.

The door opened.

The astronauts tripped on the stonework. Only the desire to live propelled them forward, step by step. Cole's vision tunneled. He knew they were sleepy and tired and their heads hurt like the Jedik-ikik were beating their heads open.

"Mellifluous," Cole said.

They reached the door and collapsed inside the small entry room. Cole remembered falling on top of someone, but he wasn't sure who. The door was still open. He reached for it. So did someone else. Was it Emily? Everything was fading.

"Story," he said, and fell unconscious.

CHAPTER EIGHT: LIFE OF THE WORLD TO COME

1

IV-104 slid into orbit around 51 Golgotha. The crew were less than half an hour from strapping into the DSMUs and beginning the final descent onto the surface of the exo-planet. But for now, Cole was content to be in the Anchor's grand cupula, enjoying a serene view of 51 Golgotha a's three moons, S 2042 G 1, G 2, and G 3, as they hovered over the Anchor like singular clouds floating across a west Texas skyline.

The grand cupula was one of the few weightless environments on the Anchor. While the living quarters and most of the ship remained under gravitational control, this part of the ship was sequestered by itself. This wing was sequestered because, as NASA psychologists had learned, astronauts missed the weightless environment and all the fun and unique experiences it provided.

Being able to float among the stars was one of the astronauts' greatest pastimes during their long voyage to the exo-planets.

Cole Musgrove was soaking up the last of bits of weightlessness, sipping his coffee from a cup specifically designed to counter microgravity while he stared at the four immense planetary bodies in his view.

A different kind of body drifted up to him and put her hand on his shoulder.

"You have that faraway look, Cole. A penny for your thoughts?" He turned and saw that she was filming him.

"I was thinking about all the great weightless sex we've had onboard the Anchor. Totally unprotected sex, so there is probably space spooge seeped into everything around here. It's a wonder the wires haven't shorted. Oh, is that thing on?"

Emily's face twisted up and she playfully slapped his shoulder. "You know it's on, and look what I can do with the press of a button: Wow, it's already deleted," she said as she pressed a few buttons, then re-aimed the lens to her husband. "So really, what's going on in that 'oh so thoughtful and articulate' head of yours?"

"I was thinking that we're the first people from our planet to be here. Those three moons, and this beautiful planet that once harbored intelligent alien life. We live in an age of miracles, Em."

"That's much better for the camera."

"Like the way you rocked my world earlier this morning. I think it's a miracle I didn't pull something." Cole faked rolling his shoulder like he had pulled a muscle. This time Emily kicked him. He would have floated backward into the cupula if not for having a grip on a handrail.

"Stop."

"We're all so very fortunate to be here, Em. We are true Lewis and Clarks, untethered from the world we know. And I'm more fortunate than anyone else here because I get to share these moments with the love of my life."

"That's the man I married."

Emily turned off the camera and snuggled into her husband. They floated curled up into each other and weightless in the cupula. Alien planets whirled around them.

That was when C.C. interrupted them. "Hate to bother you guys, but it's about time to go. We are three hours away from our seven minutes of hell. Time to suit up."

"Shh, C.C. I'm having a moment," Cole said.

"Didn't you guys already have a moment earlier?"

Emily kicked out at C.C., too. "Does everybody have to know our business?"

"If you didn't want that, maybe next time don't replace the injured linguist with your husband," C.C. teased.

"That was a decision made by the director, not me. I fought against having him here. It's bad luck to have a husband onboard a ship." She pinched her husband's cheek as she kissed him.

Cole pulled back. "Bad luck? I'm practically an American hero at this point."

C.C. laughed. "Naw, dude. You're just the language guy."

The three pushed off and floated up the wide hall to the DSMU dock. Six DSMUs (one for each astronaut and an extra) stood in Descent stage on top of large concave platforms.

2

"So we're alive, but we have no way home," Cole said.

"No, there's a way," Emily said from across the table at the Hab. "The 'Supreme Conqueror' thought he'd marooned us here when he shot down the Anchor, but NASA prepared for even that eventuality."

"I'm with you there," Cole said. "I remember that training."

C.C. said, "I think what Cole's saying is he doesn't see how we get up to the satellites to build the ship to get us back to Earth."

"Ahem," Mathieu said.

"Sorry, Mathieu."

Anna put her hand tenderly on Mathieu's shoulder.

"Just trying to point out your lack of insight when it comes to these things."

"Don't be a turd."

"It's all I've got to look forward to. Get it? I *look* forward to it." Mathieu smiled while pointing to the bandage wrapped over his eyes and around his head.

"Does this mean we have to listen to constant bad blind jokes from now on?" C.C. asked.

Mathieu recited, "I came into this world, so that those who do not see may see, and that those who see may become blind."

C.C. gave him the one finger salute.

"I see that, too."

"Aw, come on. How'd you see that?"

"Hey, look on the bright side," Anna said. "At least you don't have that problem with ocular vision degradation any more."

"Oh, I'm hurt," Mathieu said in mock disdain.

"Back to the problem at hand," Cole said. "How do we get to the satellites? The Ascent Vehicle's destroyed, and none of the DSMUs have booster capability."

Emily said, "But if we combined the DSMU rocket boosters, we could get one astronaut into orbit, and that person could reach the satellite, and then they could program the other satellites. I did the math. It works."

C.C. said, "I saw your math. It barely works."

"Barely works still works."

"What about the CEV? If we reduced the weight, we could probably get it out of Golgotha's atmosphere," Cole said.

"That could work," Emily said. "But we need fuel."

"The ISRU station?"

"That is a possibility, if we are willing to wait five months to generate enough liquid oxygen."

Cole didn't like waiting any longer. There were no ruins left. He just wanted to get home.

Mathieu said, "I think there's another way. Does anybody remember what the Supreme Dickhead said before he sent us away so that I could get worms placed in my eye sockets? He said that we were a people of the impossible because we could go into space. The Jedik-ikik could only send things into space."

Anna snapped her fingers. "The Doomsday Engine. It had exhaust ports."

"They used it to shoot the Rentok while they were still in space, and they used it to take out the Anchor. That means they must have some sort of fuel to power it. My guess is they've found a way to supercool helium, hey. All we need to do is hope that it is the right kind of fuel, and then pump it into the CEV. It should be enough to get one person back into orbit."

"I think blindness is making you smart," C.C. said.

"No. Blindness is just God's way of bringing me down to your level. I could still do all the EVAs better than any of you. I used to do them blindfolded, and it's all about muscle memory."

"Thank you, Mathieu," Emily said.

"But what about the CEV?" Cole asked. "It isn't made for atmospheric re-entry."

"But everything here is modular. It is made to fit anywhere."

3

The Hab, which stood on wheels, had several tiled segments under its floor. Each segment went to a different vehicle. Mathieu and Cole got the task of removing the tiled floor segment that was made to fit the CEV. They then carried it out to the CEV on their DSMUs and attached it.

Anna was given the role of dismantling the CEV to lighten it. She removed the seats and much of the ECLSS system.

C.C. and Emily had the task of figuring out what kind of fuel the Jedik-ikik used, and then transporting it back to the CEV. They decided to use the GEAR (it still worked) to carry an empty tank and all the supplies they could think of for transferring fuel. Its ECLSS system was compromised, but C.C. could manage in the AXES suit while Emily followed in her DSMU mech.

They moved quietly across the land and between the burial mounds of the fallen Rentok.

"Now, I can't believe I thought they were mountains," Emily said. She was looking at a specific draw that she thought was surely the leg of a Rentok.

"We were all duped into believing they were something else. Everybody at home thought they were mountains. We were looking at it the wrong way."

"We were looking for profit dollars, so we didn't see what was right in front of us."

"I'm not going to apologize for this."

"I'm not asking you to. We all were looking for something other than what it was, so we let our charts draw the picture for us rather than use our own eyes. If we'd seen anything except a squiggly upward line on a profit margin chart, we wouldn't have come so easily."

"I feel so badly," C.C. said. "I never should have listened to Titan Space. Colonization has no place here. The only way we move forward peacefully is to do it in the interest of everyone, not just in companies."

"I'm glad you see it that way. You were starting to sound less and less like the kid I knew growing up."

"You always go back to us as kids. I think you are trying to avoid our time as adults."

Emily looked away. "We promised not to talk about that."

"You cannot erase the past, Emily."

"I'm married, C.C."

"I am well aware of that, believe me."

"The only way this team works is if you and I can cooperate. That means that whatever happened between you and me in the past is null and void."

"But I will always have feelings for you. You'll always be the one who got away."

Emily hauled back and punched him. The Army Ranger easily grabbed her fist in his hand and held it in the air. She tried to pull her fist away from him, but he wouldn't let it go until he was ready.

C.C. said, "There's been something I've been meaning to ask you, but I wanted to wait until we were alone." He waited for her response. They were coming up to Ximortikrim's battered outer walls.

"Go ahead."

"Am I commander again yet?"

"Are we out of danger?"

They were both looking up at the three monsters, each over a 100 meters tall, but Renslot the largest of all three. K'tang was no longer covered in magma. To C.C., it seemed he was smiling down at him.

"Is he smiling at you?" Emily asked. "I think he likes you."

One foot at a time, the three giants followed the two astronauts across the dead city. Each footstep sent a rumble that bumped the astronauts in their vehicles. Not a soul was living in the city. If they were, they were in hiding.

C.C. and Emily searched the dome for liquid fuel propellant. Unfortunately, what they discovered was that the Jedik-ikik trapped escaping gas from the magma beneath their city. While they could trap the gases and use them for fuel, the risk of danger from so greatly modifying their rockets was more than either commander could recommend. They returned to the Hab empty-handed.

"We will just need to wait for the ISRU to mine enough liquid oxygen," Emily said.

4

The astronauts tossed in their bunks that night, the day's troubles and weighing heavily on their minds. Anna woke when she heard Mathieu cussing in the main room. An OGRA robot was talking to him in soothing tones. "You should return to bed, Mission Specialist Du Pleises."

When Anna walked out of her room, Mathieu turned his head in her direction. He was rubbing his foot.

"You okay?" she asked.

"Sorry. I didn't mean to wake anyone. I couldn't sleep."

"Nobody can, not well at least, I don't think. It's been a hard couple of days."

"My eyes," Mathieu said. "Or at least, what's left of them. They itch, like something is still in there, scratchign at the backs of my eye sockets."

"Let me look," Anna said. She reached for his bandage.

In the dark of night, with nothing but the lulling sounds of the ECLSS air pumps and the wind blowing outside. He stopped her.

"I know there's nothing in there. It just feels like it."

"We've been running from one calamity to the other so much, we haven't had time to stop and talk about what's happened. How are you doing?"

"I took my time with it. I'm moving on. We've got work to do, and I'm still a mission specialist, aren't I?"

She pulled his head in close to hers and held it there. She closed her eyes, and together they listened to the sounds of their breathing mixed with the symphony of exploration on a hostile planet.

He stood up to go back to his bunk and slipped in his socks and fell to the ground. Anna crawled down on the floor with him and put her arms around him. He didn't fight her. Within minutes, three other crewmembers were down on the floor with them, each holding the other. They had trained together and suffered together, and now when all hope of a "quick" return home was gone, the one thing they still had was each other. They were family. Closer than family.

5

Every member of the crew was a specialist in multiple fields. So while C.C. was a geologist by trade, Anna was also a very competent student of geology. While Anna was a medical doctor and accomplished surgeon, Mathieu had spent time as a medical doctor in the army. In this way, each member was as modular as their hardware.

So while the team took the night to sleep off their woes, Anna snuck out of the bundle of family. Quietly, she slipped into her AXES suit and slipped out of the Hab's backdoor.

"Where are you going, Dr. Altieri?" OGRA asked, one of her robots approaching.

"I have questions. Don't wait up."

The robot turned to go back to its station. "Oh, OGRA? Could you lay out some pillows and blankets for everyone?"

"Yes, Dr. Altieri."

As she walked away in her DSMU, she looked back at the Hab, then up to the stars. The mountains ahead were a black serrated knife edge against the moonlit night. The three moons hovered above. From within the Calvary Mountain's black silhouette, three sets of eyes opened and watched her approach.

6

The next morning, she woke the other astronauts excitedly. They had all mostly uncurled from each other, but they were nestled around the pillows and blankets OGRA had set out for them just like Anna requested.

"Get up," Anna said. "You must come see."

Groggily, the team woke up and got off the floor.

"Did you sleep at all last night, Anna?" Emily asked.

"Not a wink. I've spent the entire night exploring inside K'tang. I've learned so much. Come see."

They climbed into their AXES suits and followed her outside.

"Ta-da!" Anna said. Her arms were splayed open and upward. The three giant monsters stood over the Hab, hiding the Golgotha system's sun. Its rays passed around the monsters.

"These are our rides."

"Our...rides?" C.C. asked.

"Yes. They can get us off of the planet."

"How are they going to do that exactly?"

"They are colonizers. They were built to land and to launch."

"And then what?"

"Follow me."

She took them inside K'tang, who had a similar elevator passage up to a compartment in his head. Seeing the empty seat in the cockpit, C.C. thought of the fate of K'tang's pilot, and how close they had come to the same fate not that long ago.

Anna brought up a video playback on the monitor. K'tang, whose sharp, angular features appeared on the screen, chirped at Anna.

"We bonded last night. Emily, did you feel like you were in a womb?"

Before Emily could respond, Anna, all smiles, said, "Here, watch this." She pressed a button on the video screen.

The video showed 360-degree playback of the Rentok launching from a distant planet and breaking through the atmosphere. Once the creature left orbit, it unfurled from its back eight different wings covered in shiny scales. It reminded C.C. of fish swimming at the surface of the ocean, and their scales glinting in the sunlight. Once the wings unfurled, the Rentok flew through outer space.

"They brought the Kroern here."

"We know that," Cole said.

"K'tang, show me fuel reserves."

"Fuel reserves at 100%," K'tang responded. He had a sharp voice, like an electric guitar thrumming out a riff.

"My book is going to outsell everybody's," Anna squealed.

"What kind of fuel is it?" Emily asked. "Please say liquid oxygen."

"I'm afraid not," Anna said. "They're powered by the radiation that they collect during space flight. You think about it, it's pretty ingenious."

"But that would mean nuclear energy being blasted here?"

"I thought of that. The desert has much less life. If we lifted off from there, we'd be less likely to harm the environment."

"They would do this for us?" Mathieu asked.

"That is one of the really interesting things I've learned about the Rentok. They are like hosts in a symbiotic relationship, but these three are alive and without pilot That is where we come in."

"So, we use them to get off this rock. Then what? Back to Earth?" C.C. asked.

"No. Earth is too far for them. Even they must take shelter from radiation every so often if they are to survive the intensity of space."

"So where do we go?"

Emily said, "I've got an idea."

The others turned to her.

"Our expedition was to 51 Golgotha a. But there were many expeditions into these systems."

"Maybe we can find one in the logs."

"No need to. I memorized them all. There was an expedition to 12 Lear scheduled for three years after our departure, and 12 Lear is five light years from Earth. At the same rate of travel that we made in the Anchor, they are scheduled to arrive there 1 year from now. So we have 1 year to travel to a planet 1 light year from here. How fast do they travel?"

Anna smiled broadly.

7

They packed everything they could take with them. That ended up including the GEAR, the DSMUs, the Hab, and all the salvageable stations, including the Animal Station. Each foot had a small hanger built between the toes of the giants. These hangers acted as storage blocks for their equipment.

Anna and Mathieu got K'tang. Emily and Cole were in Renslot. That left C.C. for the magma monster.

"I know what happened to the other two pilots. What about this one?"

Anna looked down mournfully. "He died during the first battle. Since then, he's been following Renslot, who had connected to Emily. Last night, the Rentok helped me bury the pilot."

"Are you sure we can do this?" C.C. asked. "I don't see anyone with a tattoo except you, Emily. Morder of the World, remember?"

"They can still sync up with you," Anna said.

"Guys, this is amazing," Mathieu said. He was completely covered in K'tang's extensions. "I can see again! I'm never leaving this place."

In Renslot, Emily was stripping down to connect with the Renslot.

"I haven't seen you this excited in a long time," Cole said. "You're ready to get out there, aren't you?"

"I could only do this with you."

"No, I don't think so. But I'm okay anyway. I'll go down there and buckle myself in."

"Cole." She stopped him and kissed him. "We are going home to Story. It's just a little more sideways than we planned."

He buckled into his seat.

"Is everybody ready?" Emily asked.

"Goodbye, 51 Golgotha," C.C. said. "I hope I never come back."

"Renslot, let's get off this rock. Commence ignition sequence."

"Commander," the rough, gorilla voice said. "We do not need ignition."

"You can talk?"

"We are always improving our systems."

"Alright, Renslot," Emily said. "Let's see what's out there."

The three giant kaiju looked at each other. They kneeled down low, gained their strength, and jumped into the stars.

GLOSSARY

51 Golgotha a	An exo-planet seven light years from Earth. The shorthand is "51 Golgotha." It is the first planet discovered around the star 51 Golgotha. The planet has sparse jungles, long stretches of desert, dramatically tall mountains, and a few large lakes. Three moons circle 51 Golgotha a. They have been labeled S 2042 G 1, G 2, and G 3.
Anchor	See IV-104.
ARGES	Augmented Reality Global Exploration System. Allows for the DSMU pilot 360-degree viewing at all times.
Calvary Mountains	The small mountain chain along the southern edge of Ximortikrim. The mountains separate the Habitation Module from the ancient city.
CEV	Crew Escape Vehicle.
EVA	ExtraVehicular Activity.
ECLSS	Environmental Controls and Life Support Systems.
EDLS	Entry Descent Landing Shell. This is the system that transports the astronauts from the Anchor to the ground. The system comprises of the DSMU, a heat shield, and parachutes.
ESPS	Exo-Planetary Space Expedition. The Exo-Planetary Space Program (EPSP) is a NASA program for exploring exo-planets for alien life, resources, and possible colonization. The crew of ESPS 18 are on a mission to the exo-planet 51 Golgotha a.

GEAR	Golgotha Exploration Activity Rover.
ISRU	In-Situ Resource Utilization. ISRU technology harvests fuel from the ground by superheating dirt until the atoms split into gas atoms like hydrogen and oxygen. The solids are then returned into the ground, and the gas components are stored in giant tanks and pumped into the Ascent Vehicle for fuel.
IV-104	Interstellar Vehicle 104, the Anchor. Interstellar vehicles transport astronauts to earth-like exo-planets. They are robust vehicles capable of traveling between stars at near the speed of light.
JEVS	JPL EVA System. The robot custodian of the Anchor while the astronauts are on 51 Golgotha a. Also, JEVS acts as a mission control center and relays messages to Mission Data Collection in Houston.
Jedik-ikik	Homo-Insectus. The aliens who lived and died on 51 Golgotha a.
K'tang	K't'chimigalpa-kiritikikikee k'tang. A Rentok with the ability to throw lightning.
Magma Monster	The third Rentok. Magma-breather. Has no known name, but is referred to as "Zree," which is a curse word of the Jedak-ikik.
OGRA	Operational GRound Assist. Similar to JEVS, but maintains the stations on 51 Golgotha a, including the Hab and Lab Modules and many robots (both bipedal and drone) as well as the ISRU, Communication, and Animal Stations.
Rentok	The Jedik-ikik word for the giant kaiju who attack Ximortikrim. The Kroern pilots are called Rentok Reitritz, which can mean either Rider or Raider.
Renslot	The largest and most reviled of the three Rentok. Has the ability to unleash a wave of radiation across its body, which kills the Jedik-ikik trying to attack it. Other names for Renslot include Destructor of Worlds and Curse of the Cosmos.

Ximortikrim	The name of the city of the Jedik-ikik. It is surrounded by a giant, black granite wall. The sister city, Mirkitromix, was destroyed when the Kroern first arrived.
Zree	A curse word of various utility. Used by the Jedik-ikik as the name of the third Rentok. This is not an official name, but just a curse word for the monster.

ACKNOWLEDGEMENTS

As I become more and more public a writer, and more comfortable admitting to people that I write, I've been blessed with the help and support of many friends and family. I would like to thank my father, Doug Goodman, who is my first reader and my litmus test on everything I write. I hope you enjoyed this adventure, Dad. I'd also like to thank three good friends of mine who either read through *Kaijunaut* or shared a lunch discussing human performance risks due to interstellar travel, radiation shielding, and the effects of gravity on astronauts. For a book about astronauts encountering giant monsters on a distant planet, they helped me keep the story grounded in some form of reality. Where this book goes off the rails is the author's fault. Don't blame them. That said, many thanks to Abe Gutierrez, Chip Shepherd, and Dave Brown. I'd also like to thank everyone at Severed Press for helping make this book possible when it seemed impossible. Finally, I'd like to thank my family for their support, but especially my son, who could not play Minecraft while Dad was writing. The computer is all yours now (at least until I start working on a sequel).

THANKS FOR READING

I really had a great time researching and writing Kaijunaut. If you enjoyed the book, please leave a review on Amazon. These reviews not only help others pick books, but also help authors to be seen.

I am also the author of the Severed Press books Dominion and Kaiju Fall, as well as the Cadaver Dog series. If you enjoyed Kaijunaut, please check them out.

My books can be found on Amazon at:
http://www.amazon.com/Doug-Goodman/e/B00IHF1I8S/ref=dp_byline_cont_pop_ebooks_1

My website is www.douggoodman.net.

CHECK OUT OTHER GREAT SCIENCE FICTION BOOKS

ROAK
by **Jake Bible**

There are thousands of bounty hunters across the galaxy. Solid professionals that take jobs based on the credits the bounties afford. They follow the letter of the law so they can maximize those credits.

Licensed, bonded, legal.

Then there's Roak.

Deadly, unstoppable, invisible.

SIEGE
by **Gustavo Bondoni**

This is humanity's last stand. Threatened on all sides by enemies they can't fight and often can't even comprehend, the human race has taken refuge in an inhospitable corner of the galaxy. A tiny pocket of habitable space concealed by black holes and dust clouds, hiding a cluster of colonies where the last humans in the galaxy reside, preparing themselves for a war of annihilation against all comers. Crystallia is a hidden military base that guards the access route to the colonies. The main mission of the soldiers there is to remain undetected for as long as possible, to spot any incursions from the outside and to hit them with everything in humanity's arsenal. No one is quite convinced that this strategy will be enough to save the colonies or even to create enough of a delay for some of the colonists to escape. The best bet for the human race is to remain concealed. Unfortunately, something has found them.

CHECK OUT OTHER GREAT SCIENCE FICTION BOOKS

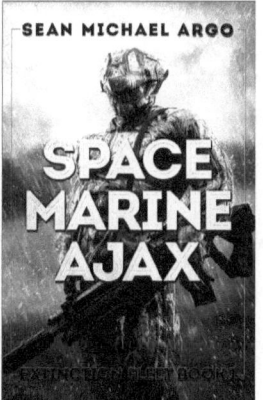

SPACE MARINE AJAX
by Sean-Michael Argo

Ajax answers the call of duty and becomes an Einherjar space marine, charged with defending humanity against hideous alien monsters in furious combat across the galaxy.

The Garm, as they came to be called, emerged from the deepest parts of uncharted space, devouring all that lay before them, a great swarm that scoured entire star systems of all organic life. This space borne hive, this extinction fleet, made no attempts to communicate and offered no mercy.

Humanity has always been a deadly organism, and we would not so easily be made the prey. Unified against a common enemy, we fought back, meeting the swarm with soldiers upon every front.

PLANET LEVIATHAN
by D.J. Goodman

The cyborg commandos of the Galactic Marines are the greatest warriors in the galaxy, but sometimes one will go bad. Too unstable to be let back into the general population and too powerful for a normal prison to hold them, there is only one place they can be sent: Planet Leviathan.

CHECK OUT OTHER GREAT SCIENCE FICTION BOOKS

DERELICT: MARINES
by **Paul E. Cooley**

Fifty years ago, Mira, humanity's last hope to find new resources, exited the solar system bound for Proxima Centauri b. Seven years into her mission, all transmissions ceased without warning. Mira and her crew were presumed lost. Humanity, unified during her construction, splintered into insurgency and rebellion.

Now, an outpost orbiting Pluto has detected a distress call from an unpowered object entering Sol space: Mira has returned. When all attempts at communications fail, S&R Black, a Sol Federation Marine Corps search and rescue vessel, is dispatched from Trident Station to intercept, investigate, and tow the beleaguered Mira to Neptune.

As the marines prepare for the journey, uncertainty and conspiracy fomented by Trident Station's governing AIs, begin to take their toll. Upon reaching Mira, they discover they've been sent on a mission that will almost certainly end in catastrophe.

ALLIANCE MARINES
by John Mierau

One by one, all of Earth's colonies have gone dark and silent. Reach, the last colony, teeters on the verge of civil war against its Earth-loyal overlords...and Reach-born rebel Lee Zhang has sworn to push the planet over the edge.

As the colony descends into total war, a convoy from Earth races across the galaxy, carrying news of a threat unlike anything mankind has faced before. The colonies have all been destroyed by a vast alien horde, and now Earth has fallen, too. Time is running out for sworn enemies to learn to trust and unite, or the human race is extinct. The Takers are coming to destroy mankind. If we don't do the job for them first.

www.ingramcontent.com/pod-product-compliance
Lightning Source LLC
Chambersburg PA
CBHW051951170626
46808CB00007B/2572